Samuel French Acting Edition

D1636657

Ken Ludwig's
The Fox On
The Fairway

SAMUELFRENCH.COM   SAMUELFRENCH.CO.UK

ISBN 978-0-573-69934-4

www.SamuelFrench.com
www.SamuelFrench.co.uk

FOR PRODUCTION ENQUIRIES

UNITED STATES AND CANADA
Info@SamuelFrench.com
1-866-598-8449

UNITED KINGDOM AND EUROPE
Plays@SamuelFrench.co.uk
020-7255-4302

Each title is subject to availability from Samuel French, depending
upon country of performance. Please be aware that *KEN LUDWIG'S
THE FOX ON THE FAIRWAY* may not be licensed by Samuel French in
your territory. Professional and amateur producers should contact the
nearest Samuel French office or licensing partner to verify availability.

MUSIC USE NOTE

Licensees are solely responsible for obtaining formal written permission from copyright owners to use copyrighted music in the performance of this play and are strongly cautioned to do so. If no such permission is obtained by the licensee, then the licensee must use only original music that the licensee owns and controls. Licensees are solely responsible and liable for all music clearances and shall indemnify the copyright owners of the play(s) and their licensing agent, Samuel French, against any costs, expenses, losses and liabilities arising from the use of music by licensees. Please contact the appropriate music licensing authority in your territory for the rights to any incidental music.

IMPORTANT BILLING AND CREDIT REQUIREMENTS

If you have obtained performance rights to this title, please refer to your licensing agreement for important billing and credit requirements.

KEN LUDWIG'S THE FOX ON THE FAIRWAY was first produced by the Signature Theatre (Eric Schaeffer, Artistic Director; Maggie Boland, Managing Director) in Arlington, Virginia from October 12 – November 14, 2010. The production was directed by John Rando, with sets by James Kronzer, costumes by Kathleen Geldard, lighting by Colin K. Billis, and sound by Matt Rowe. The Production Stage Manager was Kerry Epstein and the Production Manager was Timothy H. O'Connell. The cast was as follows:

JUSTIN	Aubrey Deeker
LOUISE	Meg Steedle
BINGHAM	Jeff McCarthy
PAMELA	Holly Twyford
DICKIE	Andrew Long
MURIEL	Valerie Leonard

KEN LUDWIG'S THE FOX ON THE FAIRWAY was subsequently produced by the George Street Playhouse (David Saint, Artistic Director) in New Brunswick, New Jersey on March 25, 2011. The production was directed by David Saint, with sets by Michael Anania, costumes by David Murin, lighting and sound by Christopher J. Bailey. The Production Stage Manager was C. Renee Alexander. The cast was as follows:

JUSTIN	Reggie Gowland
LOUISE	Lisa McCormick
BINGHAM	Peter Scolari
PAMELA	Amy Hohn
DICKIE	Michael Mastro
MURIEL	Mary Testa

FOREWORD

The Fox on the Fairway is a farce, and it was written in homage to the great English farce tradition that began in the 1880s and flowered in the 1920s, '30s and '40s.

A farce, essentially, is a broad comedy where the emphasis is more on the story and the plotting than on the emotional journey of the characters. It typically has a broad, physical, knockabout quality and is filled with recognizable characters who find themselves in precarious situations. Great farces are minutely plotted, and part of the joy we take from a great farce comes from the beauty of the play's architecture. When a complex story ticks along without missing a beat, then fits together perfectly at the end like a Chinese puzzle box, we leave the theater feeling exhilarated. The experience might be described as catharsis through laughter.

Farce on stage begins with Plautus in the 3rd century B.C. Twenty of his plays survive, and Shakespeare used several of them as sources of plot and character in the most overtly farcical of his own plays, including *The Comedy of Errors, The Taming of the Shrew* and *The Merry Wives of Windsor.* Farce recurs again and again in the history of British stage drama, from Ben Jonson's *The Alchemist* in the 17th century to David Garrick's one-act curtain-raisers in the 18th. In fact, virtually all of the comic masterpieces written at the end of the 18th century, including *She Stoops to Conquer* by Oliver Goldsmith and *The School for Scandal* by Richard Brinsley Sheridan, have strong farcical elements throughout.

The particular tradition that I'm honoring in *Fox* is a kind of comedy that first appeared in 1885-1887 in a number of tremendously success-ful comedies by Sir Arthur Wing Pinero (the first playwright in history to be knighted). These include *The Magistrate, The Schoolmistress,* and *Dandy Dick.* They are all set in upper-middle-class England amid clerics and judges, teachers and students, youngsters and oldsters, where youth ultimately fools old age and gets what it wants. Close on the heels of these plays, in 1892, appeared what is probably the most successful farce of all time, *Charley's Aunt* by Brandon Thomas. It is the zany story of an Oxford student who dresses up as his friend's aunt in order to help the cause of true love and thwart the older generation.

Beginning in 1922 the playwright Ben Travers wrote over a dozen comedies known as the Aldwych Farces (because most of them were first produced at the Aldwych Theatre in London), including *A Cuckoo in the Nest, Rookery Nook, Plunder* and *Thark.* These featured the same group of actors from play to play, involved amorous uncles, forbidding mothers, opinionated servants and innocent ingénues, and became tremendously popular with the English public. The Travers tradition was then carried on, and indeed enriched, by many of England's finest dramatists, such as J.B. Priestley (in *When We Are Married*), Terence Rattigan (in *When the Sun Shines*) and Noël Coward (in *Blithe Spirit* and *Look After Lulu*). Along the way there were some outstanding one-offs, like *Tons of Money* by Evans and Valentine, and *See How They Run* by Philip King. (P.G. Wodehouse wrote the greatest farces of all time in this tradition, and he did it for over 75 years during the first three-quarters of the twentieth century. In Wodehouse's case, however, they are in the form of novels and short stories.)

What the plays in this tradition have in common is not only their wildly funny stories and characters, but a firm sense of their own innocence. Their authors were very aware of the sex-fueled, often bitter French farces by Georges Feydeau written in the decades around 1900; but that is not exactly what they wanted to emulate. They wanted Feydeau's extravagant plots, colorful characters and breathless climaxes without the adultery and the pessimism. Thus emerged the singular tradition of British farce.

In *The Fox on the Fairway* I've tried to touch base with some of the specific characteristics of this genre to try and keep the banner flying for what I consider to be an important yet endangered tradition. For example, many of the above-mentioned classics had sporting themes, probably because professional sports have a jaunty yet competitive edge that can bring out the best (and worst) in all of us. Some of the farces in this tradition revolve around bets; many of them concern marriages on the brink of disaster; some involve authority figures brought down to earth; and all of them concern young love fighting for survival.

It is important to put this genre into its own context. If it is judged – wrongly – in comparison to emotional comedies (say *Twelfth Night* or *Private Lives*) or intellectual comedies (say *Volpone* or *Major Barbara*), critics who don't understand the genre will find it wanting in emotion and intellect. If it is judged in comparison to the edgy farces of Joe Orton and Alan Bennett (say *Loot* or *Habeas Corpus*), it will not be found savage enough. The joy of the farces by Travers and Priestley, Pinero and Thomas, is in their plotting, wordplay, rhythm and exuberance. They all have a breezy quality that is intentional. For me, these plays reach a genuine depth of artistic merit, but it is the kind of depth we associate with great technique – in painting, for example, with composition, brushwork, and the choice of subject matter. If a critic finds *Charley's Aunt* too "frivolous," then he has not entered the theater with the right critical tools.

Finally, I've written this play not only as an homage to the earlier tradition, but also as a reminder of the values that the tradition embodies, things like innocence, humor, good sportsmanship and honor. My hope is that it is still possible to come together in a darkened theater and embrace these values with a sense of joy. If so, there may be hope for us yet.

Ken Ludwig
April 2011

I encourage theaters to put this Foreward into their programs and press packets. To download an electronic copy, please visit The Fox On The Fairway *web page at www.kenludwig.com.*

CHARACTERS

JUSTIN

LOUISE

BINGHAM

PAMELA

DICKIE

MURIEL

SETTING

The Tap Room of Quail Valley Country Club, this year.

For Olivia and Jack

ACT ONE

Scene One

(We're in the Tap Room of Quail Valley Country Club on a summer's day this year. There's a bar at the back, a sofa, a chair, and a large picture window [the fourth wall] looking out on the golf course. A bag of golf clubs is propped in the corner. It's a beautiful room at a beautiful club.)

(The room has five exits/entrances. French doors upstage lead out to a patio and then the golf course. Through them we can see the 18th hole in all its glory. Stage right of the French doors is a door to a closet. Stage left of the French doors is the bar. The bar is flanked by two doors, which lead to the kitchen as well as other parts of the club, including the director's office. One or both of these doors can be swinging. Finally, down right, there is a hallway. It leads to other parts of the club, and there is a blue chair [out of sight] near the end of it.)

(As the lights come up, a sort of prologue begins involving most of our characters. It consists of a series of lines about the game of golf, which are said in motion, to the audience, as the characters begin the action of the play.)

(First, JUSTIN. He's about 25 years old, offbeat, sweet, anxious, a bundle of nerves with unruly hair. At the moment, he's excited about some news he has to deliver. He's dressed up (for JUSTIN) in a sport coat and tie, and he runs in from the outside patio.)

JUSTIN. Louise!…Louise?!

(He turns to the audience:)

As-as-as Mark Twain once said, "Golf is nothing but a good walk spoiled." *Louise?!*

9

(He runs out. LOUISE, a waitress at the club, now hurries in from the kitchen. She's a knockout – 23, leggy, good-natured, and a little ditzy. She's in her own world which is very innocent and wonderful to visit.)

LOUISE. Justin?...Justin?!...

(to the audience)

Golf is easy. The first thing you do is buy clothes that don't match.

(She hurries out. As she goes, DICKIE BELL and HENRY BINGHAM enter from opposite sides. They are the Executive Directors of rival country clubs, both in their mid 40s. They glare at each other, then turn to the audience:)

DICKIE. I'm not saying my golf game is bad but if I grew tomatoes, they'd come up sliced.

BINGHAM. Golf spelled backwards is flog. Think about it.

(As they go, PAMELA, 39, beautiful, tanned, and very sophisticated, walks through on her way to a board meeting. To the audience:)

PAMELA. Golf and sex are the only things you can enjoy without being good at them.

JUSTIN. *(off)* Louise?

(PAMELA turns and hears JUSTIN and smiles.)

PAMELA. *(to the audience)* And so we begin.

(This signals the beginning of the play proper, and the lights change. As PAMELA disappears, JUSTIN hurries into the room looking for LOUISE.)

Louise, guess what?! I have surprise for y -...
Louise?...Louise?!

LOUISE. *(off)* Justin?

(Simultaneously, as JUSTIN goes out through the door to the left of the bar, LOUISE comes in through the door to the right of the bar.)

Justin, I -...Justin?

JUSTIN. *(off)* Louise, I've got to talk to you! Our entire lives are at stake!

(She goes off through the door to the right as he comes in through the door to the left.)

Louise?

LOUISE. *(off)* Justin?!

(And he heads off through the door to the right, as she comes on through the door to the left:)

JUSTIN. *(off)* Louise?!

LOUISE. Justin, I'm in the Tap Room. I'm standing just in front of the bar near the window!

(JUSTIN enters through the door on the left.)

JUSTIN. There you are.

LOUISE. Justin! What are you doing here? And look at you, you're all dressed up. What is it?!! What's going on?!!

JUSTIN. Don't I get a kiss first?

LOUISE. Oh, sorry.

(She puts her hand on the back of his neck and gives him what looks like the best kiss of the century. It's totally unselfconscious and enormously sexy. She releases him as matter-of-factly as she kissed him and he reels backwards.)

So what's up?

JUSTIN. I'm-I'm-I'm-I have a surprise for you.

LOUISE. I love surprises.

JUSTIN. I know you do. Well, the first thing is…I-I work here.

LOUISE. Where?

JUSTIN. Here at Quail Valley. Isn't it great?! I work for Mr. Bingham. I'm his new assistant. So now we can see each other all the time!

LOUISE. *The* Mr. Bingham? As in the head of the club?

JUSTIN. Yeah. Isn't it something?

LOUISE. Justin, that's fantastic! When did you start?

JUSTIN. About five minutes ago. And I haven't even been fired yet!

LOUISE. That is so great! But how did you get the job?

JUSTIN. Well, a few days ago I-I stopped by the club to say hi, and I saw Mr. Bingham chasing some man across the ninth green, trying to hit him with a 7-iron. He was shouting "You incompetent bungler!" – so just to be funny I said, "You should use a pitching wedge so when you hit him you'll get more loft," and he turned to me and said, "Would you like a job, because any moment now there'll be an opening," and so he gave me an interview!

LOUISE. Oh, wow. Then it must have gone well.

JUSTIN. It went like a dream! I-I told him how much I love golf and I think that impressed him. I mean not that I'm allowed to play here, as an employee.

LOUISE. Did you tell him your scores?

JUSTIN. Yeah. He said what did you shoot the last time you played and I told him the truth – it was a hundred and thirty-six – and he laughed so hard that he spit up his coffee. So at least I put him in a good mood.

LOUISE. Well, I think you play very well.

JUSTIN. Thanks. *You* played for a while.

LOUISE. Not as well as you. I'm not *that* good.

JUSTIN. Aw. Anyway, he told me all about the job and said I'd have to work really hard.

LOUISE. I'm not surprised. He's tough as nails. Somebody told me he eats barbed wire for breakfast, but I said that's not possible, it's not on the menu. I also think he's unhappy in his personal life.

JUSTIN. Is he married?

LOUISE. Yeah. He calls her Lady Voldemort, She of Darkness. But you know this is tournament weekend, so if he hired you now he really must have confidence in you.

JUSTIN. Tournament weekend?

LOUISE. Yeah. Every year we play Crouching Squirrel Country Club for the Inter-Club Championship. It's a really big deal. Sort of like Troy versus Greece in the 8th century B.C.

JUSTIN. Night school?

LOUISE. We're studying the Homeric epic. I'm reading *The Iliad.* Our teacher asked us what *use* we thought it would be, studying Homer, and I said maybe picking up old blind Greek men. But he said we should compare the story to our everyday lives and this tournament has turned out to be like perfect!

"O hear thou Gods of the game of sticks
And little dimpled balls,
For thou hast pitted Crouching Squirrel
Against Quail Valley
And the greens this day are tricky!"

That's part of my term paper, I'm writing a sort of ode to golf. And Quail Valley is just like Troy cause we always lose.

JUSTIN. Always?

LOUISE. For the past five years. And Mr. Bingham gets really upset about it. Between you and me, I think he puts money on it. Muchacho dolores.

JUSTIN. Listen, I haven't even told you the *big* surprise yet.

LOUISE. You haven't?

JUSTIN. See, now that I have a full-time job, I have a salary, right? And-and you have a salary. So you see what that means?

LOUISE. …Two salaries?

JUSTIN. Right…and with two salaries, I guess we can afford to…

(He takes a ring box out of his pocket and opens it. Then he gets on one knee. Her jaw drops.)

Louise Margaret Heindbedder, will you marry me?

LOUISE. Oh, Justin! Oh! Yes! Yes! Yes! A hundred and forty-seven times yes!!

(She kisses him and hugs him and dances around the room.)

Oh, Justin! Oh look at this *ring*.

JUSTIN. It was my grandmother's.

LOUISE. Wow.

JUSTIN. It's been in my family for over 40 years.

LOUISE. Oh my God. Oh, Justin, you've made me the happiest woman in this room! Let's make out!

(LOUISE starts getting very enthusiastic with JUSTIN. She kisses him with passion and runs her fingers through his hair. Then she starts removing his belt. JUSTIN can't help responding and has his hands all over her – at which point MR. BINGHAM enters. He's carrying a framed photo of a golfer. He watches them for a moment.)

BINGHAM. ...Excuse me?

JUSTIN & LOUISE. *Ahhhh!*

JUSTIN. Mr. Bingham, I-I-I was looking for you!

BINGHAM. And you thought you might find me in Miss Heindbedder's brassiere?

JUSTIN. No. No, no. This is special!

LOUISE. He's telling the truth!

BINGHAM. You know this could be a record. Hired and fired in ten minutes.

JUSTIN. No! No sir, listen, I-I-I just asked Louise to marry me.

BINGHAM. And did she say yes or was that your consolation prize?

LOUISE. I said yes. I mean I'm in love with him!

BINGHAM. You know that's genuinely touching. I'm very moved. Inside. My giblets are doing a little dance of joy. But may I remind you that this is a country club and not a cathouse, and that if anyone else had walked through this door and seen your live demonstration of "The Kama Sutra," *I would have had to FIRE BOTH OF YOU!*

JUSTIN. I'm sorry, sir.

LOUISE. Me too!

BINGHAM. Miss Heindbedder you may go. Or would you like one last grope to keep you going until lunch time.

LOUISE. …I'm fine sir.

(She exits.)

JUSTIN. Sir, I'm-I'm very sorry, only we just got engaged, sir. Pretty soon I'll be a married man!

BINGHAM. Oh aren't you lucky. Marriage. Such a wonderful state. The state of marriage. I believe it's located above Alaska. Same climate but in my case there's no drilling allowed.

JUSTIN. Aw, you're putting me on, aren't you sir. As they say these days, "You're messing with my head."

BINGHAM. Wouldn't that be a pleasure. But no, not today, because today of all days I will let nothing spoil the fun.

JUSTIN. Is there something special happening, sir? I-I know it's Tournament Weekend.

BINGHAM. It is indeed.

JUSTIN. Do you think we have a chance, sir?

BINGHAM. "Do we have a chance?" No, Hicks, we don't have a chance. We have a shoe-in.

JUSTIN. A new member, sir?

BINGHAM. A new member indeed. The fellow's name is Tramplemain. There he is. Look at that extension. Mwa.

(He kisses the picture he carried in.)

And he is the nicest man in the entire world. He joined the club about a month ago, he's in finance, I think, plays golf as a hobby and his last four rounds were 75, 73, 76, and *71! Ha!*

(He casually takes a picture of another golfer off the wall and drops it in the trash, then puts up Tramplemain's picture in its place.)

JUSTIN. So what happens next? We just start the tournament?

BINGHAM. Not quite. In about five minutes we have the "Signing Ceremony." The Director of Crouching Squirrel, my counterpart, a man named Richard Bell, who, I might add is the lowest chiseling son of a bitch who ever walked the earth, and I say that with all due respect, arrives in one of his ugly sweaters and we sign the Tournament Book, thereby confirming the names of the players. Then he and I shake hands, I excuse myself, I wash my hand and we're off and running.

(He glances out the window.)

Ah, here he comes now. You can always tell it's him from the heavy shoes he wears. They're meant to hide the cloven hooves inside the *Dickie Bell, how are you Dickie Bell.*

*(**DICKIE BELL** enters. He's an unpleasant man full of bonhomie. He's wearing the ugliest bright yellow sweater in existence.)*

DICKIE. Hello Henry, just look at you, don't you look marvelous! A little tired, though, eh? Around the eyes? You've got to stop working so hard, old boy. It's just too late. Life has passed you by, eh? Ha ha ha ha ha ha ha!

BINGHAM. Nice sweater, Dickie. Very understated.

DICKIE. Do you like it? It's called Positano yellow, I believe.

BINGHAM. Ah yes. Italian word for vomit, I think.

JUSTIN. Hel-hello.

BINGHAM. So sorry. Dickie Bell, Justin Hicks.

DICKIE. Capital. Just capital to meet you.

BINGHAM. "Capital?" Are you English today?

JUSTIN. Would you like a drink? I-I can –

DICKIE. Don't mind if I do. So what if it's early. So's the worm. Otherwise he wouldn't catch anything.

BINGHAM. You mean the bird.

DICKIE. Sorry?

BINGHAM. You said the worm.

DICKIE. I meant the worm.

BINGHAM. No you meant the bird.

DICKIE. Didn't mean the bird.

BINGHAM. Of course you did. The early *bird* catches the *worm.*

DICKIE. Yes, but if the worm wasn't up even earlier, the bird couldn't catch him. So the worm's the early one. Right, eh? Ha ha ha ha ha ha ha!

BINGHAM. Oh that's excellent, Dickie. You could go on stage with that one.

JUSTIN. Maybe I should, uh –

BINGHAM. Yes, of course, I'll see you later.

 (*JUSTIN exits.*)

 So, Dickie, how's it going?

DICKIE. Oh I can't complain and who'd listen anyway, eh? Ha? Big day of golf ahead. Mm? Love golf.

 (*He looks out the 4th wall toward the golf course.*)

 And how's the wife? God, I love Muriel, she's such a strong woman. Like a Sherman Tank. No feet, she has treads on the bottom, churning forward over the landscape.

 (*He makes a tank-going-over-terrain noise.*)

 Keeps you in line, eh? Ha ha! Love that.

BINGHAM. I'm sure you do.

DICKIE. Now, now, it's just a joke, we can all take a joke from time to time, eh? And speaking of jokes, how's your team this year?

BINGHAM. ...I beg your pardon?

DICKIE. I said how's your golf team. Speaking of jokes.

BINGHAM. Are you honestly standing here in *my* tap room, drinking *my* liquor and insulting my club?!!

DICKIE. Now, now I didn't say you don't have a chance. It's golf, eh? Drives, chips, putts, who knows what could happen.

BINGHAM. *(bravely)* Yes, of course, you're right. In fact, just to show you I'm not a sore loser, I suppose I should put a little money on it, shouldn't I.

DICKIE. Now there I agree with you. A bit of jousterting I call it. A clash of arms. So what do you say? How much?

BINGHAM. Oh I don't know. You do have the better players of course.

DICKIE. Not necessarily! Where's your spirit? Let's hear it for Quail Valley. Chucka chucka chucka!

BINGHAM. Chucka chucka chucka!

DICKIE. So what do you say, shall we call it ten?

BINGHAM. Well –

DICKIE. Ten thousand dollars, straight up, no odds.

BINGHAM. Ten thousand dollars! Oh, I couldn't.

DICKIE. Well, if it's too much money –

BINGHAM. Let's make it twenty. I mean why not. What's a little wager between friends, hm?

DICKIE. Well now, if you're talking twenty, I suppose we should say thirty.

BINGHAM. Forty.

DICKIE. Fifty.

BINGHAM. A hundred.

DICKIE. A hundred thousand?

BINGHAM. What's the matter? Afraid, are we? Not man enough? Oh, Dickie, you disappoint me.

DICKIE. I'll tell you what. I'll go for a hundred thousand dollars on one condition. That if I lose, I'll pay you *two* hundred thousand dollars, but if you lose you pay me a hundred thousand and throw in your wife's antique shop.

BINGHAM. …Muriel's shop?

DICKIE. Muriel. Your wife. Big woman. Wears camouflage.

BINGHAM. Her antique shop?

DICKIE. Ye Olde Crock. Now I know it's not worth a hundred thousand, but I've always had a fondness for it. I like all that wood, the old tables, mirrors.

BINGHAM. But she loves that shop. She lives for it. If anything happened to it, she'd kill me. She'd murder me. I'd be a dead golfer.

DICKIE. Oh all right, I understand. Get on her bad side and she might shoot you with those swivel guns near the hatch. "A-a-a-a-a-a-a!" So let's just call it off, no bets, just golf.

BINGHAM. We can still bet the cash, of course.

DICKIE. Nah. Why bother. You know me, I don't like to go halves.

BINGHAM. Oh come on. Make it interesting. A hundred each way. Or seventy-five. Or fifty.

DICKIE. Nah. Not worth it. Cheers. I'll come back later and sign the book.

(He heads for the door and walks out.)

BINGHAM. …All right.

DICKIE. *(returning)* What's that?

BINGHAM. I'll do it. One hundred against two hundred.

DICKIE. And you throw in The Olde Crock?

BINGHAM. My wife?

DICKIE. The shop.

BINGHAM. Oh. Yes.

DICKIE. Done! Let's shake on it. Ha ha! What a man. Congratulations. You got me again, you devil. Shall we sign the bookage? Give it the old Johnny Hancocks?

BINGHAM. Oh let's. Why not. Then we'll have the whole day ahead of us just for golf.

(DICKIE signs the book.)

DICKIE. Ah, I see you have Tramplemain down here.

BINGHAM. Oh, you've heard of him, have you?

DICKIE. I've seen him play. Good man. Good short game.

BINGHAM. Oh, I think he's a little better than just "good," don't you? I'd say excellent. Or crackerjack. Wouldn't you say that?

DICKIE. Yes I would actually. But there's a problem here. With Tramplemain.

BINGHAM. Well, let's see. Did I spell it wrong? Wrong color ink? I'm sure I can fix it.

DICKIE. No, it's not that. It's just that you've got him in the wrong column. He's playing for us.

BINGHAM. …I beg your pardon?

DICKIE. Tramplemain joined Crouching Squirrel yesterday afternoon. And resigned from Quail Valley. I'm sure you'll find his letter in your mail this morning.

BINGHAM. …What did you say?

DICKIE. I said Tramplemain changed country clubs. He's playing for us now.

BINGHAM. But he can't do that.

DICKIE. Oh come now Henry, anybody can resign from one club and join another.

BINGHAM. But…but…Now wait a second! You put him up to this, didn't you?

DICKIE. Now, now.

BINGHAM. And you arranged the timing!

DICKIE. That's hardly the point –

BINGHAM. Of course it's the point! You come in here and make a bet when I think I have Tramplemain and then you…You're trying to cheat!!

DICKIE. Oh stop it, Henry. It's a free country. We have the Bill of Rights and Wrongs.

BINGHAM. Yes, but…But! Ha ha! BUT! We have *rules*, don't we? Inter-club *rules* that were written fifty years ago. Wait, they're right over here, look!

(He pulls a rule book off a shelf, then flips madly to the right page.)

BINGHAM. *(cont.)* "Except in the case of injury, you may not introduce a *new name* into the Tournament Club Book within less than twenty-four hours before start of play." Ha ha ha ha ha ha! Here it is, in black and white! We start playing in twenty minutes, Tramplemain is a new name, I win, you lose, end of discussion.

DICKIE. Well, you've got the rule correct, old man, but I didn't break it. You see we're *not* introducing a new name into the Book. Tramplemain's name is right there, it's merely in the wrong column. So we're easily within the rules, twenty-four hours, spelled correctly, in the book.

(He heads for the door and spots the mail.)

Ah, look at this. Today's mail, and there it is. From Tramplemain. See you on the links. And say hello to Muriel for me!

(He makes his tank-over-terrain noise as he exits.)

*(**BINGHAM** tears open the letter and reads it. Then sits down, weak at the knees. He starts shaking violently.)*

BINGHAM. Jesus Christ.

(He calms himself, thinks for a moment, and hurries to the phone and dials.)

Hello, *hello!*...Yes, put Roger Paisley on please. It's Henry Bingham. ...*Henry Bingham, one of his oldest clients do you need a hearing aid, you old bat?!!*...Ah, Roger, it's Henry here. I was wondering, as my banker, if you might do me a favor. I'd like to take out a second mortgage on the house and...Oh not too much, let's say two hundred thousand. Oh and by the way, make sure you don't use the Olde Crock for any of the collateral...No, not Muriel, the shop. You know Mu –...Hm? What? Say that again? Who wants to buy her shop?...But they're developers. Why would they – ?...Tear it down and put up a shopping mall? Well I'm sure she'd never agree to –...two million d -? Now let me get this straight: You say that Bell and Son Builders are offering to pay two million dollars for Muriel's antique shop so they can tear it down and…Did you say Bell and Son? That wouldn't be run by Dickie Bell, the fellow who's director of… Oh my God! So *if* let's say he won the shop in I don't know a wager of some kind, he wouldn't have to *buy* it at all, he could just… *Well why didn't you tell me all this before?!*…Well if the offer came *in* last night you should have *called* me last night!…*Yes*, I'll still need the second mortgage unless Quail Valley Country Club *burns to the ground in the next twenty minutes!*

*(He slams the phone down – at which moment, **PAMELA PEABODY** enters. She's blondly beautiful, about 39, and extremely soigné. Her clothes are impeccable and she has seen it all. Clearly she's a member of the club.)*

PAMELA. Hello, Mr. Bingham.

BINGHAM. Mrs. Peabody. How are you?

PAMELA. Oh I'm all right, but you're not so good, I'm afraid.

BINGHAM. I'm sorry?

PAMELA. I've just come from a meeting of the Club's Executive Committee. Do you want the good news or the bad news first?

BINGHAM. Bad news?

PAMELA. No, I'll start with the good news. The good news is that the committee realizes that it was not your fault that we lost the Inter-Club Cup five years in a row. The bad news is if we lose it again you're fired.

BINGHAM. They can't fire me, I'm a member of the club!

PAMELA. Not if you're fired, apparently.

BINGHAM. But I've run the club for them for the past five years.

PAMELA. Vindictive bastards, aren't they. Drink?

BINGHAM. At 10:15 in the morning?

PAMELA. I know, I got a late start.

*(She goes behind the bar and gets a bottle of brandy and pours two glasses. Meanwhile, **BINGHAM** sits down and puts his head in his hands.)*

PAMELA. *(cont.)* Look, it can't be that bad. We could still win the tournament, couldn't we? We must have some pretty good players.

BINGHAM. *(laughs hollowly)* Not good enough. It's medal play and now they have Tramplemain.

PAMELA. Tramplemain?

BINGHAM. Best player in the city. It was arranged by your ex-husband, the all-time snake in the grass Dickie Bell.

PAMELA. Snake in the grass is too kind for him. What about venomous weasel-toad jackal from hell.

BINGHAM. You had a good marriage, then.

PAMELA. *(getting caught up in her feelings)* Lying, adulterous, clawed rat-vulture from the Kingdom of Mordor.… Pissing, fly-specked, warthog-lemur from the Land of *Vomit.*

(catching herself)

Hahahahaha. These are jokes, Mr. Bingham. To cheer you up.

BINGHAM. *(tries vainly to smile)* Yes, of course…

PAMELA. Oh come now. Surely we have someone who can compete with this Tramplemain. What about that boy I just passed on the practice tee? He looks quite good.

BINGHAM. I have no idea who you're talking about.

(We hear the distant thwack of a golf ball. **PAMELA** *goes to the picture window and looks out.)*

PAMELA. There he is. He's still at it.

(Thwack.)

Look at that drive, it's straight as a die.

(Thwack.)

There's another one. That must be 300 yards. I'll bet he has incredible back muscles. Honestly, come look.

*(**HENRY** sighs and drags to the window. Thwack.)*

See what I mean? The kid's a champion.

(Thwack.)

BINGHAM. Oh my God, that's Hicks.

(calling through the door)

Hicks!...*Hicks, get in here!*

JUSTIN. *(off)* Yes, Mr. Bingham!

PAMELA. Who's Hicks?

BINGHAM. He's my new assistant. Hicks!

JUSTIN. *(off)* Coming!

(JUSTIN rushes in.)

Oh, sir, I'm-I'm-I'm so sorry! I-I-I was passing the practice tee and there was this driver lying there on the ground and I thought I'd try just one shot and-and-

PAMELA. Where did you learn to hit like that?

JUSTIN. I-I started early, I guess.

BINGHAM. What's your handicap?

JUSTIN. *My* handicap? About scratch.

BINGHAM. *Scratch?*

PAMELA. What do you shoot? Normally, on a good round?

JUSTIN. Oh I don't know...About 69 or so. I shot a 64 once at Lakeview in Connecti –

BINGHAM. Oh stop it! You told me you shot a hundred and thirty-six!

JUSTIN. I did. It was a tournament and we played two rounds. I shot a 69 and a 67. It would have been 66 but I blew the last putt. I could have killed myself. But honestly, sir, I-I-I'll do anything to make it up to you. I mean I know I shouldn't have even picked up the club, but I'm so happy about Louise and all and I –

BINGHAM. *Shut up! I need to think!* This could be...Wait a second. Are you lying to me?

JUSTIN. No, sir. Why would I –

BINGHAM. Here. Take this.

(He hands JUSTIN a putter that was in the corner, and he puts a golf ball on the carpet in front of him.)

Do you see that blue chair? Down the hall? Hit the right leg.

JUSTIN. You mean putt it?

BINGHAM. No, Hicks, I mean walk over and break it in half with your head *of course I mean putt it!!*

JUSTIN. Sorry.

(*JUSTIN has a short, eccentric pre-shot routine – he shakes one foot, then the other, etc. – then lines up the putt and hits it. We watch the ball travel across the room, through the doorway, there's a pause while the ball keeps traveling and clunk.* **BINGHAM**'s *eyes gleam.*)

BINGHAM. Do it again.

(*Same drill. Ball on the floor, swing, roll, disappears, clunk.*)

JUSTIN. *(happily)* If you'd like, I can do it left-handed.

BINGHAM. Oh my God.

PAMELA. Tell me, why aren't you a pro or something?

JUSTIN. Oh, please, I'm not *that* good. And I'm inconsistent! One round it's 69, the next round it's 66.

(**PAMELA** *and* **BINGHAM** *exchange a look.*)

See, I get upset under pressure and if something bad happens, I can go to pieces!

BINGHAM. All right, listen to me Hicks and listen *very carefully.* You are going to play for Quail Valley today in the Inter-Club Tournament and it starts in less than ten minutes! Now let me make something entirely clear. I want you to play the best golf you have ever played in your whole life. I want you – *look at me!* – I want you focused, I want you sharp, I want you at the top of your game. If you win the tournament, I'll arrange playing privileges for you here at the club year-round for the rest of your life and I'll pay for your honeymoon. *However,* if you do *not* win the tournament, I will fire you from this job, I will ruin any possible chance you have of ever marrying Louise, and you will die alone and childless without the price of a golf ball in your pocket *IS THAT CLEAR?!*

PAMELA. I thought golfers were supposed to feel relaxed before playing.

BINGHAM. *Then feel relaxed, goddamit!*

JUSTIN. *Yes sir, I'm relaxed!!*

BINGHAM. Now go to the pro shop, pick some clubs and an outfit and charge it to me.

JUSTIN. You, sir?

BINGHAM. Yes!

JUSTIN. Is there a team color I need to choose for the outfit?

BINGHAM. No, just anything, pick what you want.

JUSTIN. Blue shorts?

BINGHAM. Blue shorts are fine.

JUSTIN. And I saw this sort of red-bricky-colored polo shirt as I walked by the –

BINGHAM. *PICK WHATEVER YOU WANT, I DON'T CARE IF IT'S A SUN DRESS, JUST PUT IT ON AND GET BACK HERE!!*

JUSTIN. *Yes sir!*

(JUSTIN *runs out.*)

PAMELA. Now he's relaxed.

BINGHAM. Well I'm sorry but this happens to be very important!

PAMELA. I hate to bring this up, but doesn't he have to be elected to membership in order to play in the tournament?

BINGHAM. Good point, good point. All in favor of Justin Hicks say aye.

PAMELA. Henry, I barely know him.

BINGHAM. Pamela, *please*, I need your help! We've known each other since we were children. I've seen you through at least three ma- …

PAMELA. Three marriages? Thank you for that.

BINGHAM. No no. No. No no. I didn't say marriages. I was going to say three mmmmmarvelous terms as Treasurer of the Board!

PAMELA. One term.

BINGHAM. One term.

PAMELA. As Vice President.

BINGHAM. Vice President.

PAMELA. Is there something at stake here I don't know about?

BINGHAM. Well…

PAMELA. You put some money on it, didn't you.

BINGHAM. Yes.

PAMELA. A lot of money.

BINGHAM. Well…Yes.

PAMELA. Oh what the hell, put my name down.

BINGHAM. You're a wonderful woman. I'll go fix the books, they're in my office.

(He rushes off through the club door and **PAMELA** *watches him go.* **PAMELA** *pours herself another glass of brandy as* **DICKIE** *enters. He's still wearing his hideous sweater.)*

DICKIE. Pamela.

PAMELA. Oh my God, now I need two drinks.

DICKIE. I was about to say it's nice to see you again.

PAMELA. And I was about to say get the hell out of here.

DICKIE. Pamela –

PAMELA. Do you realize that if you'd bought that sweater *while* we were married it could have been grounds for divorce all by itself.

DICKIE. I didn't buy it, it was a free gift.

PAMELA. And that should be a lesson to you: never use box-tops to acquire wearing apparel.

DICKIE. Very funny. As it happens, I have a secret admirer who sends them to me in little brown parcels. She signs herself "Scaramouche." I was hoping it was you.

PAMELA. Oh, please, if I ever sent you a package in brown paper it would be ticking.

DICKIE. I don't know what I ever did to you that was so terrible.

PAMELA. How about sleeping with every woman in our neighborhood. You covered the entire subdivision, house by house. It was like watching Sherman march through Georgia.

DICKIE. And you were never unfaithful, I suppose.

PAMELA. Never.

DICKIE. Oh, please.

PAMELA. Never. Not once.

DICKIE. Well, I didn't mean to be!

PAMELA. You didn't mean to be 13 times?

DICKIE. You knew I had an eye for the ladies. Why did you marry me?

PAMELA. I was rebelling against my parents. They said you were a no-good, two-timing, second-rate louse but I said no you were merely dumpy, dull and delusional.

DICKIE. Well, you all got that wrong, didn't you. I believe I've made a little something of myself, eh? Hanh? Director of Crouching Squirrel Golf and Racquet Club.

PAMELA. A job which *I* got you so you'd stop living off me!

DICKIE. That was a court settlement!

PAMELA. That was highway robbery! Three thousand dollars a month.

DICKIE. The judge believed me.

PAMELA. The judge liked you for some bizarre reason.

DICKIE. Of course she liked me. I slept with her.

PAMELA. You slept with the judge?

DICKIE. Mm. And I told her you were promiscuous. She was appalled.

PAMELA. That's it! How much did you bet on this tournament?!

DICKIE. None of your business!

PAMELA. It *is* my business because I'll see to it that you lose every penny of it!

DICKIE. When the swans fly home from cappuccino.

PAMELA. Capistrano, you idiot!

(**BINGHAM** *hurries in.*)

BINGHAM. I took care of the books –

(*sees* **DICKIE**)

And oh my God, I think your sweater's gotten even louder. It seems to change color like a living organism.

DICKIE. You can both insult me all you like, but the fact is I'm about to win a tournament. Now the Starter needs to know who you're putting up against Tramplemain. I assume it's Sullivan and you're moving everybody up a notch.

(**BINGHAM** *and* **PAMELA** *glance at each other.*)

BINGHAM. No, no, it's not Sullivan. It's one of our fairly newer members. His name is Justin Hicks.

DICKIE. Right, I'll tell them.

(*He heads for the door, then pauses.*)

Justin Hicks. Isn't that the fellow I met earlier?

BINGHAM. Right.

DICKIE. I had the impression he worked here.

BINGHAM. No, no, he's a member. Full-fledged, good standing. Awfully nice fellow as it happens. Gynecologist, I believe.

DICKIE. (*suspicious*) How long has he been a member here?

BINGHAM. Oh let's see, he's fairly recent, I believe. He applied here last winter, joined up in March and now he's a member.

DICKIE. He applied last winter and joined in March?

BINGHAM. Yes, so what? That's what I said!

DICKIE. Well that's very odd now isn't it considering *that your club has a one-year waiting list for new members! Now what's going on here?! You're pulling a fast one, aren't you?!!*

PAMELA. He's my nephew.

DICKIE. What?

PAMELA. My nephew.

DICKIE. You don't have a nephew. And what's that got to do with it anyway?

PAMELA. Relatives of members don't have waiting periods, and of course I have a nephew, he's my brother's son, but you wouldn't know that because you spent the entire six months of our marriage being promiscuous to a degree unrivalled since the Age of Caligula. So I suggest that you go find one of your flexible admirers and join her on a lawn chair next to the fairway so you can watch Quail Valley beat the crap out of Crouching Squirrel, now get the hell out of here.

DICKIE. To the spoils go the victor and I intend to be one of them.

(**DICKIE** *exits.*)

PAMELA. Mr. Bingham?

BINGHAM. Yes, Mrs. Peabody.

PAMELA. You and I have a mission.

BINGHAM. We do?

PAMELA. We are going to see to it that Quail Valley wins this tournament and that my ex-husband, Mr. lying, goat-withered, can't-keep-his-zipper-up, wart-sucking adulterer from the Planet Piss-Head loses every penny.

BINGHAM. I love you.

(*At which moment,* **JUSTIN** *rushes in with* **LOUISE** *and he's wearing a brightly-colored golfing outfit – looking just as ridiculous as a full-dress golfer should.*)

JUSTIN. How do I look?! The truth?!

BINGHAM. Like a Christmas ornament. Now stand up straight!

JUSTIN. *(happily)* Up straight.

PAMELA. Chin up!

JUSTIN. Chin up!

BINGHAM. You're representing Quail Valley, young man, and I want you to go out there and give it your best no matter what!

LOUISE. Don't worry, Mr. Bingham, I know he'll win it. I gave him the best good-luck charm in the world. I kissed his balls!

(JUSTIN *beams happily.*)

It always gives him so much confidence!

PAMELA. I'll bet it does.

LOUISE. And with the help of Aphrodite, goddess of love, The Trojans spied the long par five and said "It shall be conquered!"

(*From offstage we hear the* **STARTER** *speaking over a loudspeaker, which echoes over the course. Like all Starters, he speaks in a monotone.*)

STARTER. (*off*) Ladies and Gentlemen: welcome to the 43rd Annual Golf Tournament between Crouching Squirrel Golf and Racquet Club and Quail Valley Golf and Country Club.

(*applause, off*)

BINGHAM. All right, come on, come on…what are you doing?!

(JUSTIN *is on the floor doing push-ups.*)

JUSTIN. It's part of my pre-shot routine.

BINGHAM. Not now, you idiot! Just get out there and play golf!

JUSTIN. Right-o!

(JUSTIN *and* **LOUISE** *hurry happily out the door.*)

BINGHAM. (*to* PAMELA) Are you coming?

PAMELA. I'll watch from here.

(**BINGHAM** *hurries out.*)

STARTER. (*off*) For our first match this morning we have Mr. Steve Tramplemain and Mr. Justin Hicks. Will Mr. Hicks please come forward?

BINGHAM. (*off*) We're right here! All set! No problem!

(PAMELA *wanders to the picture window in the fourth wall and looks out.*)

STARTER. *(off)* The first hole is a short par 4 playing two hundred and eighty-four yards to the front of the green. Ladies and gentlemen, please welcome Justin Hicks.

JUSTIN. *(off)* Hey, watch this!

SPECTATORS. *(off)* Go, Justin!

Go, Justin!

STARTER. *(off)* Will Mr. Hicks please refrain from doing push-ups in the tee box.

(*More laughter off – as* BINGHAM *hurries in through the door.*)

BINGHAM. I can't watch, I just can't watch.

PAMELA. Shhh!

BINGHAM. Couldn't he just act normal like everybody else?!

PAMELA. Come look. He's addressing the ball.

STARTER. *(off)* Quiet, please. Quiet on the tee.

(*Silence. Thwack. Enthusiastic cheers from the crowd:*)

SPECTATORS. *(off)* All right, Justin!

Get in the hole!

PAMELA. Oh my God, what a shot!

BINGHAM. *(hurrying to the window)* Let's see. Where?

PAMELA. There! It's heading straight for the green!

BINGHAM. Holy Hannah.

PAMELA. He could reach it in one!

BINGHAM. Come on, come on…

PAMELA. Come on, just a little farther…

BINGHAM. A little farther…

PAMELA. …*COME ON, YOU SON OF A BITCH!*

(*Thump. It lands on the green.*)

He did it. He's on the green. We could actually win this thing.

BINGHAM & PAMELA. *(scream) YES!!!*

> *(**PAMELA** has jumped onto **BINGHAM** and is straddling his stomach with her legs – and they realize it just at the moment of – blackout!)*

End of Scene

(Lively music takes us into...)

Scene Two

(That afternoon, about 6:30.)

(When the lights come up, **BINGHAM** *is alone in the Tap Room, setting up an ice bucket.)*

BINGHAM. *(singing)* "Zip ah dee doo dah,

Zip ah dee ay,

My oh my what a

Wonderful day!"

(There is a boom of thunder, and **BINGHAM** *looks up.)*

STARTER. *(off)* There will be a short rain delay, so please take shelter. After 16 holes the score remains Tramplemain at minus one and Hicks at minus nine.

BINGHAM. "Plenty of sunshine

Coming my way,

Zip ah dee doo dah

Zip ah dee ay!"

*(***PAMELA*** appears at the door in a new outfit.)*

PAMELA. You sound cheerful.

BINGHAM. *(turning)* Hello, Mrs. Peabody and oh my God you look glamorous.

PAMELA. Why thank you Mr. Bingham. I thought I should get into the spirit of things.

BINGHAM. Well that's certainly the spirit of something all right. A little champagne? De petit caviar?

PAMELA. Aren't we counting our chickens a bit?

BINGHAM. With an 8-shot lead on the 17th? It's true, of course, golf being so dangerous, that he might run afoul of the famous wild gophers of the 18th green.

*(***PAMELA*** laughs – at which moment **DICKIE** enters.)*

DICKIE. Ah, Bingham—I was hoping to catch you. Hello, Pamela.

PAMELA. Richard.

DICKIE. Now listen, Bingham, I have a deal for you that you can't refuse. Now there is no doubt in my mind that this Justin Hicks of yours is a put-up job, but I will permit the game to go forward to its natural conclusion provided we call off the bet. Now you certainly can't ask fairer than that!

(**BINGHAM** *laughs in his face and happily leaves the room.*)

DICKIE. Bingham! Bingham, listen to me!

(**DICKIE** *runs after him. As he goes,* **LOUISE** *enters from the kitchen carrying a tray with snacks, which she starts distributing around the room.*)

PAMELA. Hello, Louise.

LOUISE. H-hi...

(*Sniff. There's a catch in her voice and she wipes a tear from her eye. She's been crying. She starts refilling all the nut and snack bowls but she's pouring so much that the bowls overflow and there are nuts everywhere. She barely notices. She's so distraught that she can hardly breathe.*)

PAMELA. Louise, is something the matter?

LOUISE. N-no.

(*sniff*)

Not really. I mean it's nothing important, I'm sure it will...it'll-it'll –

(*She starts to cry.*)

PAMELA. Oh, Louise dear, sit down. Can you talk about it?

LOUISE. (*haltingly, through her tears*) It's just that I...I...*I lost my engagement ring!!*

PAMELA. You lost it?

(**LOUISE** *nods, unable to speak.*)

Are you sure?

(*Nod, nod.*)

LOUISE. *(gasping for air)* I – I was in the bathroom and the ring was loose – I told Justin it fit perfectly but it didn't – and as I was flushing the toilet, I pushed the handle and it fell off into the water *and I flushed my engagement ring down the toilet!!*

PAMELA. Louise, calm down –

LOUISE. *The toilet!!*

PAMELA. *Louise!!* Just listen! Now this is a very big day for Justin and I think you should wait to tell him about it. He has a lot on his mind right now.

LOUISE. Oh, I know that, Mrs. Peabody, and I'd never say anything to him in a million years. I mean, when you get to know him better, you'll see that if he gets upset about anything, he goes right off his game.

PAMELA. …Really?

LOUISE. One time last summer his mother called him in the middle of a round because she had the flu and he-he got so upset he spoiled a 12-point lead in like three holes.

PAMELA. But how could he – ?

LOUISE. He just whacked at the ball like he didn't care. You see, he's very close to his mother.

PAMELA. I see, but –

LOUISE. And I can understand how he feels because I was a foster-child and for a while I didn't even have a mother –

PAMELA. Yes, I see, but –

LOUISE. Though I'll admit that his mother can really get on my nerves sometimes –

PAMELA. *Louise!* I understand. But you're not going to tell him, right?

LOUISE. Right. I'll just keep it all bottled up inside –

(sob)

PAMELA. Good.

LOUISE. And I won't tell *anyone.*

(sob)

PAMELA. Excellent.

LOUISE. Unless he asks me *and then I won't be able to stop myself!*

(She bursts into tears and runs from the room.)

PAMELA. Louise!

(She starts to run after **LOUISE** *when – Ring! It's the telephone. She hesitates for a moment – then grabs the phone.)*

Yes?!

(Squawk!)

Hold on…Mr. Bingham?

BINGHAM. *(off)* Yes?

PAMELA. Your wife's on the phone.

BINGHAM. *(off)* Tell her I'm not here!

(Squawk, squawk!)

PAMELA. She says she heard that.

*(***PAMELA** *puts down the phone and runs after* **LOUISE**. *The moment she's through the door,* **BINGHAM** *enters from the kitchen and picks up the phone.)*

BINGHAM. Now how on earth could you possibly hear that, Muriel? You must have the ears of a Cherokee Indian.

(Squawk, squawk!)

No, I *like* the Cherokee, Muriel. They're very good trackers. We have one as a member and he hasn't lost a ball in ten years.

(Squawk!)

What's that?

(Squawk, squawk, squawk, squawk!)

Yes, I heard you! There's a package being delivered here, priceless vase *for* the store, you won't be *at* the store, you're having a facial and would therefore miss the delivery and I'm to guard it with my life. *Got* it!

(Squawk! Squawk!)

You too, dear, good-bye.

*(He hangs up – at which moment, **JUSTIN** appears at the door to the course. He's carrying a golf club.)*

JUSTIN. Hi, Mr. Bingham.

BINGHAM. Justin! What are you doing here?!

JUSTIN. There's a rain delay.

BINGHAM. Oh right, right, right, of course. Come in. Well.

(He takes a breath and smiles broadly.)

Justin.

JUSTIN. Mr. Bingham.

BINGHAM. Justiiiiiiin.

JUSTIN. Mr. Binghaaaaaam.

(They both laugh happily and slap each other. It's a guy thing.)

BINGHAM. What can I possibly say, young man, but *well done!*

JUSTIN. Thank you, sir.

BINGHAM. Have a cigar.

JUSTIN. I don't smoke, sir.

BINGHAM. Then have two so you can practice.

JUSTIN. Thank you, sir.

BINGHAM. Now Hicks, I want you to use this rain delay to relax and prepare yourself mentally for the final hole.

JUSTIN. Yes, sir.

BINGHAM. I want you to focus and think about nothing but golf. Now close your eyes. Remember, Hicks, golf is not a game, but a way of life. A religion, if you will, with its rules and traditions, its customs and its practices. It says that life is noble and never slovenly. It says that life has grandeur and deeper meaning. It is the game of Sam Snead, of Arnold Palmer and of Jack Nicklaus.

(Both men cross themselves.)

BINGHAM. *(cont.)* It began, of course, with the ancient Egyptians, who used sticks to strike the heads of their enemies. It then reemerged in Scotland in the year of our Lord 1450 at the Royal and Ancient Golf Club of St. Andrews. At the time, the balls were covered in goat-skin, the players had a mere four clubs to choose from, and the caddies were little drunken Irish people, but at least it was a start; and I want you to think about these traditions as you visualize the putt ahead of you on the 17th green. I want you to *feel* it as the club swooshes like a parabola through the crisp, clean air. Golf is Zen and Zen is Golf. You are a Buddhist now Hicks. Ommmmmmm.

JUSTIN. Ommmmmmm.

BINGHAM. This day is called the Feast of Crispian.

JUSTIN. It is?

BINGHAM. No, you idiot. That's Shakespeare, to inspire you.

JUSTIN. Oh, sorry.

BINGHAM. Ommm.

JUSTIN. Ommm.

BINGHAM. This day is called the Feast of Crispian. We few. We happy few. We band of brothers. Ommmmmmmm.

JUSTIN. Ommmmmmmm.

BINGHAM. Are you ready now, Hicks?

JUSTIN. I think so, sir.

BINGHAM. Are you going to *win?!*

JUSTIN. *Absolutely, sir!*

BINGHAM. Let me hear the Quail Valley cheer! Chucka, chucka, chucka!

JUSTIN. Chucka, chucka, chucka!

BOTH. *(like a steam train building speed and power)* Chucka, chucka, chucka! Chucka, chucka, chucka! Chucka, chucka, chucka! Chucka, chucka, chucka, chucka, chucka, chucka!! *To victory!!*

(The telephone rings. JUSTIN answers it.)

BINGHAM. No, don't!

(Squawk!)

JUSTIN. Sir, it's your wife.

BINGHAM. *Yes,* Muriel?

> *(Squawk!)*

Yes, I said I would check with the front desk, wait a moment, it's call waiting.

> *(Click.)*

Yes?...Thank you, I'll be right there.

> *(Click.)*

That was the front desk, Muriel, the package is here, I'll go sign for it.

> *(Squawk, squawk!)*

Fine, come see it whenever you please!

> *(hangs up; to* JUSTIN*)*

I'll be right back.

> *(pinching* JUSTIN*'s cheeks)*

What a smile!

> *(BINGHAM exits. JUSTIN is pumped. He marches around the room in triumph humming Hail To The Chief. Then LOUISE enters with a tray.)*

JUSTIN. Dee-dee-dee-dee, dee-dee-dee-dee-dee-dee-dee-dah!!...Louise!

LOUISE. *(hiding her left hand)* H-hi, Justin.

JUSTIN. So what do you think?! Are you proud of me?

LOUISE. Are you kidding? I'm-I'm like busting my buttons just watching you out there.

JUSTIN. Gee, thanks.

> *(LOUISE tries to go about her work, but since she can't use one of her hands, she uses her elbow and shoe to try and clear the tables of the nuts she's spilled.)*

LOUISE. And I'm-I'm really glad that there's nothing going on to distract you and all.

JUSTIN. Thanks.

LOUISE. Cause you've got to keep focused, right? So you don't think about other things like...

(sob)

JUSTIN. What?

LOUISE. Like personal stuff that isn't important right now and...

(sob, sob)

JUSTIN. What's the matter?

LOUISE. Nothing. I-I-I just got a cough or somethin', I'm sure it'll just...

(bravely)

Let the games commence
While Troy and Greece are
Locked in mortal...locked in...

(Sob. She tries to smile. Sob. She tries again, but this time the dam bursts and she really lets it out.)

Oh, Justin!!

JUSTIN. What is it? Louise, what's the matter?!

LOUISE. *(crying her eyes out)* I'm sorry, Justin! I didn't mean to cry in front of you. It's just that I love you so much!

JUSTIN. Louise, just tell me! Is it my mother?!

(She shakes her head no.)

Is it the dog?!!!

(No!)

Is it something I did or said or...

(He notices her finger.)

Hey wait a second. Where's your ring?

(She shrugs, unable to speak.)

Did you lose the ring?

(She nods.)

JUSTIN. *(cont.)* Are you sure?

(Nods.)

Oh my God.

LOUISE. Oh, Justin, I'm so sorry! I think I - ...I think I... flushed it down the toilet!

JUSTIN. Oh my God! That was Granny's ring!

LOUISE. I know! It was too loose and it just came off!

JUSTIN. You said it fit!

LOUISE. I said it to be nice!! And I shouldn't have worn it! AND I WAS STUPID!!

(*At which moment,* PAMELA *enters and sees* LOUISE*'s hysteria.*)

PAMELA. Oh my God. What's going on?! Oh no, you told him.

(JUSTIN *is so distraught he makes gurgling sounds or hisses.*)

LOUISE. No. Yes. I didn't mean tooooooo!

JUSTIN. (*literally climbing the furniture*) Oh my God...

PAMELA. Justin, it's all right!

JUSTIN. But it was Granny's ring!

LOUISE. Grannyyyyyyy's!

PAMELA. Justin! You can buy a new one.

JUSTIN. You're right, you're right. I'll buy a new one. It'll be fine.

LOUISE. Are you sure? It won't be Granny's.

JUSTIN. Oh that's all right. These things happen. We'll get a – we'll get a *used* one. It'll be *somebody's* Granny's. Ha ha ha.

LOUISE. You promise?

JUSTIN. Yeah.

LOUISE. Oh, Justin! I love you *so much!*

(*They embrace and weep and wail.*)

(PAMELA *watches them and begins to get teary.*)

PAMELA. You two really have something going, don't you?

(*sob*)

But I guess we all need a little...

(*sob*)

A little...

(She breaks down and starts weeping. This just encourages **JUSTIN** *and* **LOUISE** *to go back at it, and now all three of them are wailing like an Irish family at a wake, weeping and screaming and hugging each other.)*

(At which moment, **BINGHAM** *bounds happily into the room with the package.)*

BINGHAM. And how's my *happy* little *golfer*?!

(They look up and stare at him...and burst again into wails of anguish.)

What the hell is going on here?!

LOUISE. Just say you forgive me, Justin, that's all that matters.

JUSTIN. Louise, I forgive you.

LOUISE. Are you sure?

JUSTIN. Absolutely. Of course, I'm not going to loan you my car after this, heh, heh, heh...

(This is greeted with stony silence.)

LOUISE. ...What did you say?

JUSTIN. I said I'm not going to loan you my...car. I was being funny.

LOUISE. That was a mean thing to say, Justin.

JUSTIN. I-I-I didn't mean it that way. Honest.

LOUISE. Does this mean you don't trust me now, Justin?

JUSTIN. Of course I trust you. I-I-I'd trust you with anything.

LOUISE. Except your car.

JUSTIN. No. Yes. No! I mean I don't want to lose it or anything, who would, but that's not the point!

LOUISE. I can't believe it!

JUSTIN. Now wait a –

LOUISE. How can you *say* that?!

JUSTIN. But I didn't m –

LOUISE. *Justin, stop it! Just-just-just stop it!* I can see that I have some thinking to do, and-and maybe this whole marriage thing is just...just...

(She bursts into tears again and rushes out of the room.)

JUSTIN. LOUISE! STOP! I DIDN'T MEAN IT! LOUISE!!

*(He tries to run after her, but **BINGHAM** intercepts him and holds him as **JUSTIN** struggles to get by.)*

BINGHAM. WHAT HAPPENED?!

PAMELA. She lost her engagement ring.

BINGHAM. Already?

PAMELA. Don't ask.

JUSTIN. Oh my God, I am so stupid! Stupid, stupid, stupid, stupid!!!

(He tries to break his club in half and then starts hitting himself in the head with it.)

BINGHAM. Justin, stop it!…Look, let's all calm down, all right?!

PAMELA. Mr. Bingham –

BINGHAM. This is obviously not *that* serious –

PAMELA. Mr. Bingham –

BINGHAM. And certainly not something that we can't put right if we just –

PAMELA. Louise just told me that when Justin gets upset like this he loses twelve strokes at a time.

BINGHAM. *(weak in the knees)* Ahhh.

PAMELA. You talk to Justin, I'll talk to Louise.

BINGHAM. Good plan.

*(**PAMELA** hurries out after **LOUISE**.)*

PAMELA. Louise!

BINGHAM. Justin!

JUSTIN. How could I even *say* that, Mr. Bingham? I mean I-I just get so wrapped up in golf sometimes that I don't even *think* straight! I should be banned from the game, that's all. I shouldn't even be allowed to play again because I'm just not fit to – Wait! That's it! I know what to do!

(He strides for the door to the course.)

BINGHAM. Wait! What?! What?! Wait! Stop! Stop! What are you doing?!

JUSTIN. I'm going to forfeit the match.

BINGHAM. NO! Justin, listen to me! That isn't necessary! Look, I'm sure she'll forgive you. You've just got to make her happy, right? Now what makes a woman happy? Hm?

JUSTIN. Love?

BINGHAM. No.

JUSTIN. Trust?

BINGHAM. No!

JUSTIN. What?

BINGHAM. An expensive present.

JUSTIN. Really?

BINGHAM. Absolutely. All right, all right, let's think. A present, a present, what can you give her…

(His eye lights on the box he just brought in.)

I've got it. Look at this. My God, she'll love it.

(He takes the vase out of the box.)

There. Look. Is that gorgeous?

JUSTIN. It's a vase.

BINGHAM. Exactly.

JUSTIN. Gee, I-I-I don't know. I mean, it's really pretty. Is it Ming Dynasty?

BINGHAM. I'm sorry?

JUSTIN. Ming Dynasty. I've heard that's famous.

BINGHAM. Exactly. That is exactly right. My God, you have an eye for these things.

JUSTIN. Gee, thanks. Look here, on the bottom, it says "London, 1847."

BINGHAM. And there you have it. Nineteenth Century English Ming Dynasty. It is very rare.

(At which moment, LOUISE comes hurrying through the room, followed by PAMELA.)

PAMELA. Louise!

LOUISE. I'm going home now.

JUSTIN. Louise, listen!

LOUISE. Justin I'm sorry but I want to go home and think this over.

JUSTIN. Wait! Look! I-I-I bought it for you, as a present, to say I'm sorry.

(He shows her the vase.)

LOUISE. ...You bought this vase for me?

JUSTIN. Yeah.

LOUISE. You picked it out?

*(***JUSTIN*** glances nervously at ***BINGHAM***.)*

JUSTIN. Yeah.

LOUISE. Gee, it's beautiful.

JUSTIN. It's Nineteenth Century English Ming Dynasty!

LOUISE. Wow. Justin, this was really...hey wait a second. It's got a sticker in here. It says...ten thousand dollars?!

JUSTIN. Ten thousand d –

LOUISE. Justin, you can't afford ten thousand dollars!

JUSTIN. Well no, I-I-I-

LOUISE. Did you steal it?

JUSTIN. No of course not! It's-it's Mr. Bingham's. He gave it to me.

PAMELA. You gave it to him?

BINGHAM. I gave it to him.

LOUISE. So you didn't pick it?

JUSTIN. Well, I-I-I picked it after he gave it to me.

LOUISE. *(in shock)* So you lied to me?

JUSTIN. Not really, I-I-

LOUISE. Justin, I can't believe this! You're just trying to *buy my affection?!* Okay, I'm outa here. Now I'm really mad.

JUSTIN. Well, well, well *fine!* Then, then, then *go ahead!* Because you're being *unfair!*

LOUISE. *I'm* being unfair?! Who made fun of who, Justin? Who had a good laugh when my heart was breaking?

JUSTIN. I wasn't having a good laugh, I-I was tired after playing a golf match that I had to play so I could keep my job and pay for the wedding!

LOUISE. Oh that is such a lie! You were doing it for the fun of it!

JUSTIN. I was not!

LOUISE. It's a *game*, Justin! It's not like pouring concrete onto a steel girder!

BINGHAM. Children…

PAMELA. If we could just say a few –

JUSTIN & LOUISE. Shut up!

LOUISE. I'm going home now, Justin.

(LOUISE grabs the vase and heads for the door.)

JUSTIN. Hey put that down!

LOUISE. It's mine, you gave it to me!

JUSTIN. Well I take it back!

(He grabs the vase and they struggle for it, pulling it back and forth.)

LOUISE. You can't!

JUSTIN. It's Mr. Bingham's!

BINGHAM. Would you two be careful!

(LOUISE has the vase now and runs out one of the kitchen doors – and JUSTIN runs after her, followed by BINGHAM and PAMELA.)

JUSTIN. Hey, come back here with that!

LOUISE. It's mine!

JUSTIN. No it's not!

BINGHAM. Justin!

PAMELA. Louise!

JUSTIN. Stop!

BINGHAM. Stop!

(By this time, LOUISE has led them back into the room through the other kitchen door.)

LOUISE. Oh here, you take it!

*(She tosses the vase to **PAMELA**.)*

PAMELA. Ah! I don't want it!

*(She tosses it back to **LOUISE**.)*

BINGHAM. Would you two stop that!

*(The vase now gets tossed around and hidden and passed like a football until it finally ends up in **BINGHAM**'s hands.)*

LOUISE. *Fine! I'm leaving!*

JUSTIN. You can't leave, I want to talk about this!

BINGHAM. Justin!

PAMELA. Louise!

(The chase continues – out the hallway right, outside past the French doors, back through the kitchen and into the room again.)

JUSTIN. I can walk out too, you know!

BINGHAM. No you can't, you have one more hole to play!

PAMELA. You know, I'm doing this in high heels.

(back in the room:)

BINGHAM. Ah!

PAMELA. What?!

BINGHAM. Look!

PAMELA. Where?

BINGHAM. Window!

PAMELA. Why?!

BINGHAM. Sunlight!

PAMELA. Sunlight?

BINGHAM. Sunlight!

PAMELA. Therefore?

BINGHAM. Rain delay!

PAMELA. Rain delay?

BINGHAM. The rain delay will be over any second!

BINGHAM & PAMELA. AHHH!

*(At which point, **LOUISE** and **JUSTIN** reenter – and **LOUISE** crosses the room and goes out the door with finality.)*

LOUISE. Good-bye, Justin!

*(**LOUISE** exits, slamming the door behind her.)*

JUSTIN. She's gone!

BINGHAM. Justin –

JUSTIN. She's gone! She's gone! SHE'S GONE!

BINGHAM. *(to **PAMELA**)* For God's sake do something!

PAMELA. What can I do?!

BINGHAM. Make him happy!

PAMELA. I only know one way to make a man happy.

(She starts pulling her dress off.)

BINGHAM. There isn't time for that!

PAMELA. Justin. *Justin!*

*(He looks up – and **PAMELA** kisses him soundly on the lips to calm him down. At which point, **LOUISE** reenters.)*

LOUISE. And I want to say just one more th-! *AHHH! JUSTIN!*

JUSTIN. *I didn't do anything, it wasn't me!*

LOUISE. Is that what's been happening? You've been seeing Mrs. Peabody?!

JUSTIN. No, I swear!

LOUISE. Justin, how *could* you?!

JUSTIN. It wasn't me! She was using my lips!

LOUISE. If that's how you want it, the engagement is *off!*

JUSTIN. *No!*

*(At which point, **PAMELA** puts her arms out and starts groping around as if suddenly blind.)*

PAMELA. Oh my God...it's happened again. I can't see! *I can't see!*

(She walks a few steps, her arms out in front of her, and stumbles into something.)

LOUISE. What is it?

JUSTIN. What's the matter?!

PAMELA. Sometimes when I-I get very excited, I'm struck with...with this condition called hysterical blindness... and it struck me just now as I was kissing Henry.

LOUISE. Henry?

JUSTIN. Henry?

LOUISE. But Mrs. Peabody, you weren't kissing Mr. Bingham. You were kissing Justin.

PAMELA. Oh, stop it.

JUSTIN. You were! It's true! It was me!

PAMELA. You're joking. Oh my God, I am so sorry!

LOUISE. *(to JUSTIN)* Then you aren't seeing Mrs. Peabody?

JUSTIN. Of course not.

LOUISE. *(to PAMELA)* But why would *you* be kissing Mr. Bingham?

PAMELA. ...Because we love each other!

BINGHAM. Oh, darling, that was our secret!

PAMELA. Oh, Henry, darling, where are you?! *Where are you?!*

(She flails her arms around trying to find him.)

BINGHAM. I'm over here, darling.

PAMELA. Oh, Henry, darling!

(PAMELA has managed to find her way to BINGHAM and she falls into his arms. Her hand feels blindly over his face.)

BINGHAM. Oh my poor darling, has it struck again?

PAMELA. I'll get through it, darling.

BINGHAM. Darling, you're so brave. You see, Pamela and I have been seeing each other for several months now.

LOUISE. You have really?

PAMELA. Absolutely.

BINGHAM. At nights.

PAMELA. On weekends.

BINGHAM. Sometimes before breakfast.

LOUISE. Aw.

(At this moment, as **BINGHAM** *and* **PAMELA** *are holding each other,* **MURIEL** *appears in the doorway but no one in the room sees her. She's a sturdy woman with a porkpie hat.)*

BINGHAM. Ever since we fell in love.

LOUISE. But what about your wife?

BINGHAM. My wife? Oh, Muriel. …I'm afraid she's dead.

LOUISE. Oh my God!

JUSTIN. I'm so sorry.

LOUISE. What happened?!

BINGHAM. Poor old girl. She just dropped in her tracks like an old horse. But I know she would have wanted me to find happiness with…

(He sees **MURIEL.***)*

AHHHHH!

LOUISE. Mrs. Bingham!

BINGHAM. Muriel! You're alive!

MURIEL. That's right, Henry. I'm still alive, and wondering *what* the *hell* you're *talking about* and *what* the *hell you're doing!!*

(And with each emphasized word, she hits him with a newspaper she's carrying.)

BINGHAM. I can explain!

MURIEL. Well you'd better start explaining right- …is that my vase?

JUSTIN. He gave it to me!

MURIEL. He *gave* it to you?

BINGHAM. Well–

MURIEL. *(hitting him with the newspaper again) What* are you *doing giving* him my *vase?!*

*(***DICKIE** *enters.)*

DICKIE. Bingham. Pamela. Oh hello, Muriel.

MURIEL. Dickie.

DICKIE. Just thought I'd let you know that the rain delay is over for the moment, so we might as well get on with this thing. I don't know what you're so angry about, Muriel. You should be celebrating. Assuming they win, you'll get to keep your antique shop.

MURIEL. "Keep it?" Why wouldn't I keep it?

DICKIE. He didn't tell you?

BINGHAM. This is a funny story, actually…

DICKIE. He bet your shop on the outcome of the tournament.

MURIEL. *What?! WHAT?! My shop?!*

PAMELA. Dickie, you son of a –

> (*And she hauls off and gives* **DICKIE** *a solid right to the jaw, which sends him to the floor, unconscious.*)

LOUISE. *Ah!*

PAMELA. (*rubbing her fist*) Ow…AH!

> (*Then she remembers: She throws her arms out, pretending to be blind again. Too late.*)

LOUISE. Oh my God! You're not blind! That was a lie!

PAMELA. Well it was, but –

LOUISE. Justin, that means you lied about everything! Good-bye!

> (**LOUISE,** *in tears, runs across the room and out the door, leaping over* **DICKIE** *as she goes.*)

JUSTIN. Louise!

> (**JUSTIN** *follows her at a run, also leaping over* **DICKIE** *– but* **BINGHAM** *throws himself in front of the door, stopping* **JUSTIN** *from leaving.*)

BINGHAM. *Stop!*

STARTER. (*off, through the outdoor sound system*) Ladies and Gentlemen: Play will now resume for all golfers in the tournament. You have five minutes to report to your positions.

BINGHAM. All right, Hicks, now pull yourself together.

JUSTIN. I don't want to play!

BINGHAM. Of course you do! It's a *game! It's fun! It's fun!*

(**MURIEL** *helps* **DICKIE** *to his feet.*)

MURIEL. You poor thing.

DICKIE. My nose!

BINGHAM. Be quiet!

MURIEL. Henry, leave him alone! This is all your fault!

BINGHAM. It may be my fault, Muriel, but if Hicks loses the match, you lose your shop!

(**MURIEL** *drops* **DICKIE** *on the floor with a thump.*)

DICKIE. Ow!

MURIEL. I don't know how you could have been so stupid, Henry.

PAMELA. He did think he had a sure thing, Mrs. Bingham.

MURIEL. You be quiet! I'll deal with you later, Peabody!

PAMELA. Oh really? Well, why don't you deal with me *right now.*

MURIEL. I'll be happy to! Husband stealer!

(**MURIEL** *shoves* **PAMELA.**)

PAMELA. *(shoving her back)* Husband oppressor!

(*They keep shoving.*)

MURIEL. Trollop!

PAMELA. Harridan!

MURIEL. Slut!

PAMELA. Nag!

BINGHAM. Muriel, stop it!

MURIEL. Henry, shut up!

JUSTIN. *(at the bar)* Maybe I shouldn't get married after all.

(*He takes a drink from a bottle of brandy.*)

BINGHAM. *Nooo!* Don't drink that, you idiot! You need to be sharp!

(They struggle with the bottle.)

JUSTIN. I said I'm not playing.

BINGHAM. You are playing.

JUSTIN. No, I'm not.

BINGHAM. Yes, you are.

MURIEL. *Young man, put that down!*

> (**MURIEL** *barks at* **JUSTIN** *with the whip-like ferocity of Herman Goerring playing a drill sergeant.* **JUSTIN** *jerks to attention at every order.)*

Stand up straight!

Pick up your club!

Now march out that door and win that tournament!

> (**JUSTIN** *starts to march out.* **HENRY** *begins to follow, but* **MURIEL** *barks him down:)*

Henry! Stay here! You upset him!

BINGHAM. But Muriel –

MURIEL. *Stay!*

> *(She marches* **JUSTIN** *out over* **DICKIE** *'s body.)*
>
> *(From offstage, we hear the spectators:)*

SPECTATORS. *(off, chanting)* Hicks! Hicks! Hicks! Hicks!

Look, there he is!

It's Justin Hicks!

Yay!

STARTER. *(off, through the speaker system)* Players, to your places, please! Play will resume momentarily.

> (**PAMELA** *is at the picture window looking out to the fairway.)*

PAMELA. Look, there he is and oh my God, Muriel is still with him. She's frog-marching him to the green.

> *(During the following,* **DICKIE** *gets up and watches the action through the window with* **BINGHAM** *and* **PAMELA**.*)

BINGHAM. Oh please let him make the putt. Just make the putt…

PAMELA. Henry, look! Justin's broken away from Muriel!

BINGHAM. Oh, no! *WAIT!* That's his driver. He's taking his driver out!

PAMELA. But that doesn't make sense. He's on the green.

BINGHAM. He's setting up for a full swing! He's lining up with the lake!!

PAMELA. What do you mean?!

BINGHAM. *He's going to hit the ball in the lake!*

PAMELA. No, no, no, no…

BINGHAM. Don't do it, don't do it, don't do it…

(*PAMELA takes BINGHAM's hand.*)

PAMELA. *(calling out) Justin, don't do it!*

(*Thwack!*)

(*beat*)

(*Splash!*)

STARTER. *(off)* Justin Hicks, scoring penalty, ladies and gentlemen, we have a whole new ball game!

BINGHAM. *NOOOOOO!*

DICKIE. *YES!*

(*blackout*)

(*music*)

End of Act One

ACT TWO

Scene One

(We're in the Tap Room that evening about 9:00. In the center of the room is now a table for two with an elegant place setting at each side, glittering with fine china, crystal, silverware and candlesticks.)

(Also in the room now is a microphone on a stand connected to a large amplifier which is plugged into the wall and connected in turn to wires leading outside. This is part of the club's rather primitive sound system for making outdoor announcements.)

(At the moment, there's a party in progress on the patio outside the tap room [through the French doors]. We see party lights through the windows and we hear sounds of chattering laughter, clinking glasses and a dance band playing in the distance. Whenever the French doors open during the scene, these noises get louder.)

(Once again, as in the opening of the play, the first scene of the act begins with a kind of prologue that starts the action. It begins as JUSTIN *hurries across the stage carrying his tux over his arm. He stops half way across the room and says to the audience:)*

JUSTIN. Hank Aaron said it took him 17 years to get 3,000 hits in baseball, but he did it in one afternoon on the golf course.

(He hurries off just as MURIEL *and* DICKIE *enter from opposite sides of the room. They look at each other, then turn front:)*

MURIEL. When I die, bury me on the golf course so my husband will visit.

DICKIE. My ex-wife bought me a book to help my golf game: Tennis for Beginners.

*(As they hurry off, **LOUISE** hurries in from a different door. She carries her evening dress with her.)*

LOUISE. One minute you're bleeding, the next minute you're hemorrhaging, the next minute you're painting the Mona Lisa.

*(As she goes, **BINGHAM** hurries in from the hall. He's wearing a tuxedo, has just been looking for **JUSTIN** and is frustrated and angry.)*

BINGHAM. For me, it's a good day of golf when I don't fall out of the cart.

*(At which point **PAMELA** enters from the kitchen dressed beautifully for the evening and carrying two wine glasses.)*

PAMELA. They say that golf is the most fun you can have without taking your clothes off. I say why choose.

*(The lights change and the play resumes immediately with **BINGHAM** and **PAMELA** still on stage. **PAMELA** is arranging the table.)*

Did you find Justin?!

BINGHAM. *(as if just entering the room)* I did.

PAMELA. Thank God!

BINGHAM. He was at his mother's house, still fairly hysterical, rending his garments like something out of the King James Bible. I told him to get the hell down here or I'd fire him on the spot!

PAMELA. I'm sure that relaxed him.

BINGHAM. Well, I don't care! It's all so simple! The score is tied, he has only one hole left to play and all he has to do is focus!

PAMELA. Easier said than done.

BINGHAM. You're telling me. I can't believe we're giving him dinner. I'd rather strangle him.

PAMELA. Do you want to win the bet or don't you?

BINGHAM. Yes, yes, yes, all right, I know. We get Justin and Louise back together, they have a night of paradise, he wakes up happy and plays like a champion. What are we feeding them, by the way?

PAMELA. Raw oysters, goose liver paté, steak tartare and figs in cream.

BINGHAM. Good God.

PAMELA. I figure they'll end up married or dead.

BINGHAM. Champagne?

PAMELA. As much as possible.

(He pours a round. She drains her glass.)

BINGHAM. Cheers.

(He knocks his back and pours another round.)

PAMELA. That's rather good. What is it?

BINGHAM. Dom Perignon.

PAMELA. Good man. I used to date him, I think.

BINGHAM. *(sniffing the champagne)* Quite fruity.

PAMELA. You're telling me.

(They knock back another. He keeps pouring.)

You know, I would drink water instead but there's all those fish in it.

BINGHAM. Dangerous.

PAMELA. Dangerous.

BINGHAM. And this is healthier, it kills germs.

PAMELA. Salut.

BINGHAM. L'chaim.

(They knock it back.)

PAMELA. The third one's always the roughest. You do know that the Golf Channel is coming tomorrow morning.

BINGHAM. What? No. Why?

PAMELA. Because we're news. At least in the golf world. "Unknown amateur golfer heading for a 64 in local tournament blows an 8-stroke lead on a single hole with only one hole left to play?" It could have been written by Puccini.

BINGHAM. *(noticing the vase)* Oh my God, what's Muriel's vase still doing here?

PAMELA. I suppose we forgot about it in all the excitement.

BINGHAM. Well, we'd better put it away before the next disaster.

(BINGHAM puts the vase into an empty champagne box and sets it aside.)

PAMELA. And you'd better tell that crowd out there that the tap room is off limits tonight.

BINGHAM. Oh. Right. I almost forgot. And this stupid amplifier never works.

(He takes the microphone from the stand and taps it. It comes on.)

Oh good.

(As he walks to the French doors the microphone starts to squawk with feedback.)

Oh, damn.

(He taps it and it stops squawking.)

That's better.

(He goes out towards the patio as he starts his speech.)

Good evening, may I have your attention, ple…

(The microphone starts squawking again.)

Oh, hell. Come on!

(He taps the microphone some more.)

There it is. Ladies and gentlemen, may I please have your…Damn!

(More feedback. He comes back in the room and kicks the amplifier, then gets a bullhorn out of the closet and opens the doors.)

The old standby.

(He heads for the patio again, turning on the bullhorn as he goes. Inadvertently he hits the emergency button and it starts screaming like an ambulance. He hits the

right setting and at last gets to the patio and starts the speech.)

BINGHAM. *(cont.)* Good evening and welcome to our Annual Summer Dinner-Dance and Awards Banquet to Celebrate the Inter-Club Tournament between ourselves here at Quail Valley and our esteemed guests from Crouching Squirrel.

RIVAL GUESTS. *(off) Quail Valley!*

Quail Valley!

Crouching Squirrel!

Crouching Squirrel!

BINGHAM. Thank you, that was very touching, but for now let's hold off on the drunken antagonism, if you don't mind.

("Booo!" "Yaaay!")

Now as you can see, the PA system is out of order, but I'm sure we'll have it up and running soon.

("Oh sure!" "Good luck, Henry!")

Now if I may, a couple of announcements. First, the tap room where I'm standing is off-limits tonight, but there are bars situated every 20 yards along the fairways, so we should be able to accommodate the most alcoholic among you.

("Yaaaay!")

Second, I hope you'll all join us tomorrow morning for the final hole between our own Justin Hicks,

("Hey, hey!!")

who should be here any minute, and Mr. Steve Tramplemain – there he is, hello, Steve –

(applause)

who betrayed all of us here at Quail Valley, presumably for a little payola. Or a call girl.

TRAMPLEMAIN. *(off) Hey, now wait a second!*

BINGHAM. Just kidding, just kidding, it's all in fun, and best of luck to Traitor Steve. *Traitor!*

(He closes the door.)

PAMELA. I thought you handled that well.

BINGHAM. Thank you.

(LOUISE enters from the clubhouse in the sexiest red dress on the face of the earth.)

LOUISE. Hi, Mr. Bingham.

BINGHAM. Hello, Louise! Are you ready for your big night?

LOUISE. I think so. And Mr. Bingham, I-I just want to say how sorry I am about this afternoon. I know I flew off the handle, and I didn't mean to, but it was like I couldn't help myself –

PAMELA. Listen, it's a big step, deciding to get married, and it made you nervous, which is only natural. People don't get married all the time. Except in my case, and I averaged about once a year.

BINGHAM. *(glancing out the window)* Wait a moment, there's Justin. Justin!...I'll bring him in.

(BINGHAM hurries out to the party.)

LOUISE. It's nice of you to loan me your dress, Mrs. Peabody.

PAMELA. I call it my Hail Mary dress.

LOUISE. Hail Mary?

PAMELA. You save it for the final pass and if they pull it off, it's a touchdown.

LOUISE. Do you name all your dresses?

PAMELA. Most of them.

LOUISE. And what's yours called?

PAMELA. This is my Home Sweet Home dress.

LOUISE. Aw. Because there's no place like it?

PAMELA. And the front door is always open to visitors.

LOUISE. I think I'll stick to Hail Mary.

PAMELA. Well believe me, darling, if I could fill it the way you do, I'd have it glued to my body.

LOUISE. Aw, that's not true. Mr. Bingham thinks you're much prettier than I am.

PAMELA. Why do you say that?

LOUISE. Well, at the Spring Dance I overheard him tell someone that you're the most beautiful woman at the club.

PAMELA. Really?

LOUISE. Uh huh. Of course he'd just had three martinis, so it might have been the liquor talking.

PAMELA. Thank you, Louise.

LOUISE. Oh my gosh, hold it! One of my earrings is missing! I'll be right back.

(She runs out through the door to the club.)

PAMELA. Louise. Louise, it doesn't matter – !

(She runs out after her. At which moment, **BINGHAM** *and* **JUSTIN** *enter from outside.* **JUSTIN** *is wearing a rather threadbare tux, and* **BINGHAM** *is full of bonhomie for* **JUSTIN***'s sake.)*

BINGHAM. This way, this way. Ah, here we are. Good old Tap Room. Like an old friend, eh? And how are you feeling?

JUSTIN. Oh I don't know. I-I guess I'm worried about Louise and-and what she thinks of me after what I –

(deep breath)

Golly! If I could just relax the way I do at my yoga class. Do you take yoga, Mr. Bingham?

BINGHAM. No, I'm afraid I've never –

JUSTIN. Ommmmm.

BINGHAM. Ommmmm. Oh, I see, it's like I was doing bef –

JUSTIN. *Ommmmm.*

BINGHAM. Ommmmm.

JUSTIN. I am now a butterfly and my body is weightless and I am flapping gently in the warm summer breeze. Ommmmm.

BINGHAM. (*Indian accent*) Ommmmm. You are my assistant playing golf at club and if you lose I kill you.. Ommmmm.

JUSTIN. Mr. Bingham!

BINGHAM. Sorry, *sorry!* It just slipped out. Here.

(*He sits* JUSTIN *at the table.*)

How do you like our little spread? Rather romantic, wouldn't you say? Champagne?

JUSTIN. …Hey. Wait a second. Is this dinner for me and Louise?

(*i.e. the dining table*)

BINGHAM. (*modestly*) Well, it's just a little something that Mrs. Peabody and I –

JUSTIN. No.

BINGHAM. What?

JUSTIN. I-I don't want to have dinner with Louise.

BINGHAM. Why not?

JUSTIN. Because I know she hates me now and she'll think I'm trying to buy her affection again.

BINGHAM. But that's ridiculous. You want to apologize, and what could say it better than a little goose liver and steak tartare –

JUSTIN. No, I really can't. This is just too important to take a chance of -…I-I-I'll be outside.

(*He hurries out.*)

BINGHAM. Justin! *Justin!*

(*He runs out after* JUSTIN *just as* LOUISE *and* PAMELA *reenter through the club door – and therefore overhear the following:*)

BINGHAM. (*off*) Justin get back here! This is the right thing to do!

JUSTIN. *(off)* No! I don't care what you say! I'm not having dinner with Louise!

(LOUISE starts hiccupping with little sobs.)

PAMELA. No, don't. ...Don't...

(But LOUISE can't help herself. Her lip starts quivering like mad – and she bursts into tears and runs out of the room.)

Louise...Oh, Louise!

(At which point, BINGHAM marches back in.)

BINGHAM. Lord, give me strength! Were we like this when we were youngsters?

PAMELA. Are you kidding me? I'd have been up to the figs in cream by this time.

BINGHAM. Slancha.

PAMELA. Prosit.

(They each grab a bottle of champagne and hurry out of the room.)

BINGHAM. Justin!

PAMELA. Louise!

(DICKIE hurries in through the club door, followed closely by MURIEL. DICKIE is wearing a tuxedo with an outlandish, patterned vest. Or he might even be wearing an outlandish tuxedo. Whichever it is, it reflects his hideous taste.)

MURIEL. Dickie, please!

DICKIE. No, Muriel.

MURIEL. Would you listen to reason!

DICKIE. I have listened, Muriel. I don't want to talk about it.

MURIEL. But Hicks and Tramplemain are *even* now, so you should call it quits!

DICKIE. I have a funny feeling that Mr. Hicks is not quite over his histrionical behavior.

MURIEL. But if he is, you lose all that money.

DICKIE. And if he isn't, I acquire an antique shop.

MURIEL. That is so unfair! You know how I feel about that shop. I built it from nothing to fill an emptiness inside me.

DICKIE. Well I'm sorry, Muriel, but a wager's a wager.

MURIEL. We once meant something to each other, Dickie. When we were youngsters at this very club. We met at that Dinner-Dance. You wore a boutonniere.

DICKIE. You wore a tuxedo.

MURIEL. You had a moustache.

DICKIE. You had sideburns.

MURIEL. Do you remember our first date together?

DICKIE. Of course I remember.

MURIEL. We saw that documentary about the Luftwaffe.

DICKIE. I loved that film.

MURIEL. You said you found all that efficiency very inspiring.

DICKIE. I did, I *did*. Some of those babies could drop twenty tons in a single night.

MURIEL. Boom.

DICKIE. Right on target.

MURIEL. Boom.

DICKIE. And look at you. You've barely changed at all.

MURIEL. Oh, stop it.

DICKIE. You may have put on a bit of poundage, but it's all in the right places, eh? Ha? Hahahahaha!

MURIEL. Oh you devil. You always had a way of bringing out my feminine side.

DICKIE. Did I, Muriel?

MURIEL. Something my husband has completely lost sight of. He married me for my warmth, but he doesn't see it any more.

DICKIE. The brute.

MURIEL. Don't call him that. It's not his fault.

DICKIE. He is a brute if he can't see how warm and gentle you can be when you're –

MURIEL. *I SAID PUT A SOCK IN IT! Now will you call off the bet or not?!*

DICKIE. *No!*

(*They stare at each other angrily, then suddenly kiss each other ferociously. When they break it off,* **DICKIE** *has a split-second of indecision: call it off or not. He decides not, and turns and strides from the room.*)

DICKIE. No, no, no, no, no, no, no…

MURIEL. *Dickie, get back here!*

(*She runs out after him. Immediately* **LOUISE** *marches in through one kitchen door as* **JUSTIN** *runs in through the other. In surprise they see each other. Then they speak simultaneously:*)

LOUISE.	**JUSTIN.**
I realize you don't want to see me after what happened and all – !	I'm sorry if I'm just making things worse by seeing you again and – !

JUSTIN. What did you say?

LOUISE. I said I can understand if you never want to see me again.

JUSTIN. See you again? Louise, I want to see you all the time!

LOUISE. You do? After I lost Granny's ring?

JUSTIN. Of course I do! That was just an accident. And I was so unfair about the car and all.

LOUISE. Oh, that doesn't matter. I was just bein' psychosomatic or somethin'.

JUSTIN. Really?

(*She nods.*)

Do you want to go talk about it?

LOUISE. I'd love to, if it's all right with you.

BINGHAM. (*off*) *Justin?!*

PAMELA. *(off) Louise?!*

JUSTIN. Quick! This way! Hurry!

> (**JUSTIN** *and* **LOUISE** *hurry into the kitchen – as* **BINGHAM** *and* **PAMELA** *rush in still carrying their champagne bottles.)*

PAMELA. *Louise?!*

BINGHAM. *Justin?!*

> *(They see each that* **JUSTIN** *and* **LOUISE** *aren't there – and they're both ready to explode.)*

PAMELA. I can't believe it! I went to all this trouble!

BINGHAM. *(overlapping)* They are being ridiculous!

> *(Beat. They look at each other…and break into laughter. We realize now that they're both pretty tipsy. They both take hefty swigs from their respective champagne bottles and flop down next to each other on the sofa.)*

PAMELA. Oh, the hell with it.

BINGHAM. I give up.

PAMELA. All this fuss over a little game with a ball.

BINGHAM. Justin could win this thing standing on his head.

PAMELA. Here, here!

BINGHAM. There, there!

> *(They toast each other with their bottles and drink deeply.)*

Are we getting drunk?

PAMELA. Probably. I never could hold my liquor.

BINGHAM. Me neither.

PAMELA. Two, three bottles and I start to feel it.

> *(They clink their bottles and drink again. They are definitely three sheets to the wind by this time.)*

BINGHAM. I'm going to lose my shirt, aren't I.

PAMELA. I have no idea. To tell you the truth, I know very little about golf. You play, don't you?

BINGHAM. Mm.

PAMELA. Are you any good?

BINGHAM. Well, I wouldn't rename The Masters after me, but I get around.

PAMELA. "Here we are at Augusta National for The Binghams…"

BINGHAM. Ha!

PAMELA. I wonder, do you think you could give me a golf ball lesson some time? I've always wanted to play the game, but I never had the slightest idea how to go about it.

BINGHAM. Oh, oh, oh, as they say in England, you are in the right pew Madame.

(He goes to the golf bag in the corner and gets what he needs for the demonstration.)

Let's start with the basics.

PAMELA. That sounds enchanting.

BINGHAM. First, the equipment.

PAMELA. Equipment.

BINGHAM. Club.

PAMELA. Club.

BINGHAM. Ball.

PAMELA. Ball.

BINGHAM. Two balls.

PAMELA. Don't go there.

BINGHAM. Sorry. Now I need a tee. A tee, a tee, a tee…A tee you see is made from a tree.

PAMELA. And it stings like a bee if it hits you in the knee.

(They laugh at this.)

BINGHAM. Lie down.

PAMELA. I beg your pardon?

BINGHAM. Lie down on the floor. This is very instructive.

(PAMELA lies down on the floor.)

PAMELA. Are you sure about this?

BINGHAM. Positive. Now pucker.

PAMELA. Pucker?

BINGHAM. Pucker.

(She puckers her lips, and **BINGHAM** *puts the ball on her puckered lips. Then he stands back and starts waggling the club as if he's going to hit the ball off the top of her lips.)*

Wait, wait, wait, I do it better when I'm blindfolded.

(He puts his pocket handkerchief over his eyes and waggles again.)

Don't worry, I'm an excellent shot.

PAMELA. *(taking the ball off her lips)* I'm counting on that.

BINGHAM. Put it back.

(She puts the ball back on her lips and closes her eyes as he waggles the club. He pulls the club into his backswing…when suddenly she sits up and cries out:)

PAMELA. *Ah!*

(He swings through, just missing her head.)

BINGHAM. *Ah! What is it?! What happened?!*

PAMELA. I fell asleep and I had a nightmare. I dreamt my three ex-husbands went on a golfing weekend and I was the seventh hole.

BINGHAM. Oh your poor thing, get up, get up.

(The music changes to a Latin rhythm and **PAMELA** *dances to the table.)*

PAMELA. Ooh, I like this music.

BINGHAM. Do you?

PAMELA. Mmm. Oyster?

BINGHAM. No thank you.

PAMELA. I love oysters.

(demonstrating:)

I love the way they slide right off the shell and into your oh my God.

BINGHAM. What's the matter?

PAMELA. It went down my dress.

BINGHAM. You're kidding.

PAMELA. *It went down my dress!*

BINGHAM. *Oh no! That's terrible! Take if off immediately!!*

> *(He grins happily at her. She gives him a look. Then she wiggles and wriggles and jumps up and down with her legs apart – and the oyster falls out.)*

PAMELA. There it is.

BINGHAM. I don't want to talk about it.

PAMELA. Alas, poor oyster. I knew him, Horatio.

BINGHAM. Would you like to dance?

PAMELA. With Oyster Woman?

BINGHAM. Do you have a super power?

PAMELA. I can make a pearl.

BINGHAM. I'll chance it.

> *(They dance. He does a fancy move and as she responds, she pulls her jacket off and throws it aside. Her dress is now quite bare on top and we see a birthmark on her shoulder.)*

Good Lord, you have a tattoo on your shoulder. That's very sexy.

PAMELA. Sorry to disappoint you but it's a birthmark.

BINGHAM. Really? It looks like a small purple flower.

PAMELA. It runs in the family. We call it the Purple Pimpernel. I have an identical, rather larger version of it on my backside and no, you're not seeing it.

> *(The song ends and we hear clapping outside.)*
>
> *(Almost without realizing it, they have become very romantic by this time and they almost kiss. They back off.)*

BINGHAM. It's getting to be banquet time and I have to speak. I'd better fix this ridiculous amplifier.

PAMELA. And if you can't fix it, we know whose fault it will be.

BOTH. Tramplemain's.

(They laugh. By this time, BINGHAM is holding the microphone, since in a moment he's going to make an announcement.)

BINGHAM. …Mrs. Peabody, can I tell you a secret?

PAMELA. Of course.

BINGHAM. I had a crush on you when we were children here at the club together.

PAMELA. Well that's a coincidence. I had one on you, too.

BINGHAM. Oh, I don't believe you.

PAMELA. It's true, I'm afraid. I remember exactly when it started. You had just come off the ice hockey rink and one of your skates was stuck and you asked me if I'd help you pull it off.

BINGHAM. I remember that!

PAMELA. One strong pull and I was yours forever.

BINGHAM. Well, why didn't you tell me?

PAMELA. Why didn't *you* tell *me?*

BINGHAM. Because I was a boy! I had acne from my chin to my forehead. I was a body and a neck with a pimple on top.

PAMELA. We did have that one date.

BINGHAM. That was much later.

PAMELA. Graduation night, as I remember.

BINGHAM. Mrs. Peabody. I think there's something I should tell you.

*(**BINGHAM** puts the microphone down on the table with a thump…AND THIS SOMEHOW MAKES THE SOUND SYSTEM COME ALIVE. We can now hear the following dialogue echoing outside in the distance on the outdoor loud-speakers. **BINGHAM** doesn't notice because he's so caught up in what he's saying. **PAMELA**, however, starts to pick up on it much earlier.)*

I think I may just possibly be in love with you.

("love with you, love with you, love with you…")

PAMELA. *(hearing their voices outside in the distance and looking around confused)* Mr. Bingham...

BINGHAM. There are many nights when I go to bed thinking of you sitting stark naked at the end of the mattress.

("the mattress, the mattress, the mattress...")

PAMELA. Mr. Bingham – !

BINGHAM. Or I dream about you tearing your clothes off one by one while pretending to resist my urgent advances –

("advances, advances, advances...")

PAMELA. *Please, Mr. Bingham -!*

(By this time, **PAMELA** *has figured out that the microphone is the culprit and she tries to turn it off – then drown it in the ice bucket, then put it up her skirt – anything to get it to stop broadcasting.)*

BINGHAM. Parading every inch of your oiled, naked body in front of me – and then belly-dancing in front of the fire!

("the fire, the fire, the fire...")

PAMELA. *Would you listen to me – !*

BINGHAM. I dream of burying my head in your chest and stroking your –

PAMELA. *Mr. Bingham, you have got to stop!*

BINGHAM. *Why?! Why must I stop?! Because I'm too old to have a little joy in my life?! Because life has passed me by before I've had any fun?! Because I'm married and therefore my life is at an end?! Is that why I have to stop?!*

PAMELA. No, you have to stop because the microphone is on.

("on, on, on, on...")

BINGHAM. AHHHHHHHHHHHHHHHHHHH!

(And now we hear applause and whistles from the party outside.)

How could you let me go on like that!?

PAMELA. *I tried to stop you but you wouldn't listen! Now turn it off!*

(*He wrestles with the amplifier and the microphone.*)

BINGHAM. *Come on, come on…It won't turn off!*

PAMELA. *Let me see it!*

BINGHAM. *There's nothing to see! Just pull the plug! Pull the plug!*

PAMELA. *I pulled the plug!!*

BINGHAM. Testing, testing…*Wait! It's still on!*

PAMELA. *How could it still be on if I pulled the plug?!*

BINGHAM. *I have no idea, it must have a battery, but why would it have a battery!!!*

(*He wallops the amplifier and kicks it and mauls it – *)

(*at which point* **MURIEL** *enters.*)

Muriel. How nice to see you.

(*Their voices are still echoing across the great outdoors.*)

MURIEL. Turn it off!

BINGHAM. We're trying!

PAMELA. It won't turn off!

MURIEL. Oh it won't turn off? Then maybe I can turn it off. *DO YOU WANT TO SEE ME TURN IT OFF??!!*

(*She picks up the driver and starts beating the amplifier with it.*)

This is how we'll turn it off, Henry!!

(*More whistles and cries of approval from outside as* **DICKIE** *comes through the door.*)

DICKIE. Two women have fainted and one man is laughing so hard he fell into the water hazard.

(*At which moment,* **LOUISE** *and* **JUSTIN** *run in from the kitchen with their clothes askew – indeed, partly removed – as though they've just been making out heavily.*)

CHEF ANTOINE. (*off*) *Get out! Get out! Zis is my kitchen!*

JUSTIN.
  Ah! We didn't mean to!

LOUISE.
  We're sorry! We got carried away!

PAMELA. What's going on?!

LOUISE. Chef Antoine just found us in the kitchen!

(embarrassed)

We were only celebrating...

BINGHAM. Celebrating?

JUSTIN. Mr. Bingham, why didn't you *tell* me that Louise forgave me?!

BINGHAM. I tried to!

JUSTIN. Well you didn't say so! But she does, and now we're getting married again!

LOUISE. Eeee!

JUSTIN. And just you wait for tomorrow morning! I'll-I'll decimate Tramplemain! I'll play the eighteenth hole like it's never been played in the history of the club!

*(He takes the club from **MURIEL** and sets up behind the champagne carton – the one that contains the vase.)*

Watch this!

BINGHAM. Nooo!

*(**JUSTIN** takes a full swing and connects with the carton – and we hear the crash of the vase inside.)*

*(At which point **JUSTIN** grabs his right arm and starts screaming:)*

JUSTIN. *Ow! Ow! My arm! My arm!*

LOUISE. *Justin!*

JUSTIN. *I think I broke my arm! Ahhhhh!*

BINGHAM. *I'll kill him! I'm going to kill him!*

*(**BINGHAM** grabs **JUSTIN** and starts strangling him. Everyone tries to pull **BINGHAM** off.)*

DICKIE. He broke his arm! He broke his arm!

BINGHAM. I'll kill him!

LOUISE. Mr. Bingham, stop it!

PAMELA. Henry!

LOUISE. Mr. Bingham!

PAMELA. Call an ambulance!

MURIEL. *(who has by now figured out that her vase was in the box – she opens it and sees the shattered remains.)* AHHHHHHHHHHH!

(At the height of the chaos: Blackout.)

End of Scene

(music)

Scene Two

(The next morning, about 8:45. Bright sunlight streams in through the window.)

(On the bar there is now a silver tournament cup with handles. It will go to the winning club and have the club's name engraved on it.)

(BINGHAM, alone, is on the phone, agitated. He still wears his tux from last night, but it's been slept in.)

BINGHAM. *(into the phone)* Hello…Hello!

(looks at his watch)

Oh, good, is this Suburban Hospital?…Yes, I'd like to speak with the emergency room. …Yes, I'm sure they're busy, that's why they call it the emer –…Yes, this *is* an emergency. …No, I don't need an ambulance, we've already had one, I just need to speak with someone in *the emergency room!…Well I don't mean to raise my voice, but you are the fifth person I have talked to at Suburban Hospital!* Yes, I'll hold!

(MURIEL hurries in. She has changed clothes.)

MURIEL. Any word on Justin?

BINGHAM. Not yet. Louise is still with him, I *think*, but I haven't heard from her.

MURIEL. It's bad enough he had to break my vase, he had to break his arm, too.

BINGHAM. We don't know his arm is *broken*, Muriel, it could be a sprain, in which case he could still finish the tournament.

MURIEL. And there could be a tooth fairy, but he's in the witness protection program.

BINGHAM. All I'm saying is that he *might* –

MURIEL. Don't speak to me! I've had enough of your delusional rantings for one weekend!

(PAMELA hurries in, also changed. She's carrying a spiral notebook and a pencil.)

PAMELA. Any word on Justin?

BINGHAM. No, I'm trying to get some word but they keep putting me on What? Hello? Is this the Emergency Room, I'm calling about a Mr. Justin Hicks.............. *OH NO!*

MURIEL. *What is it?!*

PAMELA. *What happened?!*

BINGHAM. It's the cafeteria! *Would you please just give me the…*Forget it. I give up.

(*He hangs up the phone.*)

PAMELA. Where's Louise?

BINGHAM. I'm not sure. She's supposed to call.

MURIEL. Well, she'd better hurry up about it! The match resumes at nine o'clock. That's in fifteen minutes!

PAMELA. Which is why we need to pick a replacement. I started making a list at home.

(*i.e. the notebook*)

MURIEL. "Replacement?" There are no replacements in golf! What are you talking about?!

PAMELA. (*getting the book*) Just because I knew you were going to be a pain in the neck, I took the liberty of looking it up. Under the inter-club rules, "either team may nominate a replacement for any competitor who is injured before the end of play."

MURIEL. That's ridiculous.

PAMELA. It may be ridiculous, but it's in the book. This is not the PGA, the rule is meant to foster friendly competition, it gives us one last chance to win, so I suggest that you stop complaining about it and *focus on the other members of the club! Harry Teter!!*

BINGHAM. Low 90s.

PAMELA. James Davidson.

BINGHAM. Moves the ball with his foot when he thinks no one's watching.

PAMELA. Herzberg.

BINGHAM. No long game.

PAMELA. Williams.

BINGHAM. No short game.

PAMELA. Stilwell.

BINGHAM. No game at all. Look, none of these people can replace Hicks. They're not good enough. I went through all of them before I found Tramplemain.

(DICKIE walks in.)

DICKIE. Good morning, Quail Valley!

(He's wearing another of his famous sweaters, and this is the loudest and ugliest of them all. To go with it he wears bright paisley pants.)

PAMELA. Did you have to kill it, or did it crawl onto your chest and just give up.

MURIEL. I like his sweater.

DICKIE. Thank you, Muriel. Well, well, well, what have we here? Shall I call it The Crouching Cup? You know that will look awfully nice in my lobby next to its little brothers and sisters. Love family. Oh dear, you all seem rather gloomy this morning. Not feeling so jaunty, are we Bingham, now that the sock is on the other shoe, eh?

BINGHAM. You mean the shoe is on the other foot.

DICKIE. Sorry?

BINGHAM. You said the sock.

DICKIE. I meant the sock.

BINGHAM. No you meant the shoe.

DICKIE. Don't mean the shoe.

BINGHAM. Of course you mean the shoe, it goes on the foot!

DICKIE. Ah, but you cannot have a shoe without a sock, so there is no difference.

BINGHAM. Of course there's a difference! It's called the *English language.* It has to do with communicating in an orderly fashion and not saying every piece of drivel that happens to come spilling out of your mouth!

DICKIE. Oh, oh, oh, a bit touchy are we? Nerves a bit frayed? You should have taken my little offer of yesterday, eh? Called off the bet. A bird on the wing is worth two in the air? Eh? Hm? Hanh?

BINGHAM. I'm simply not answering you.

DICKIE. Well you'd better say something, because you have ten minutes to choose a replacement for Hicks or you lose the game. Now it seems to me that you might as well forfeit and save us all a bit of time, I suppose that's up to you. Yes? No? Fine. You have ten minutes.

(He starts to exit.)

I wouldn't blame yourself too hard. You can't make straw without bricks.

(He exits. **MURIEL** *lets this sink in. Then she picks up two bottles of champagne and a plate of food and says:)*

MURIEL. I'll go talk to him. See what *I* can do.

(She walks out after **DICKIE.***)*

PAMELA. Martin Schneiderman.

BINGHAM. I just want to say, before the prow of the boat shoots heavenward and the entire ship hits bottom, that I appreciate all your efforts on my behalf. Even after last night, which gave new meaning to the term "drunken embarrassment." You're a brick, as the English say. A shot in the arm. I would now sing "You're The Top" by Cole Porter but I'd be arrested under the musical cruelty act.

PAMELA. Are you finished?

BINGHAM. Yes.

PAMELA. Martin Schneiderman.

BINGHAM. Chokes when he's ahead.

PAMELA. _____ _____.*

BINGHAM. He's never ahead.

PAMELA. _____ _____.

BINGHAM. He died over Christmas but he still might be our best prospect.

PAMELA. *(throwing the list on the table.) You'd think there'd be somebody on this Goddamn list!*

(**LOUISE** *hurries in from outside.)*

LOUISE. Hi!

BINGHAM. Well?!

PAMELA. How is he?!

LOUISE. Not so good. His arm's broken – they said it was a freak accident – and he's on so many pain killers, he's acting crazy! He's incoherent! He's like flying out the window!

BINGHAM. Tell him to move over, I'll join him.

LOUISE. Any luck with a replacement?!

PAMELA. No.

LOUISE. Geez, it seems incredible. I mean it's not like everybody in the world doesn't play golf these days. You'd think there'd be *somebody* here at the club.

(They all sit gloomily and sigh. They're at their lowest ebb.)

What about you, Mr. Bingham?

BINGHAM. My last round was a hundred and four.

PAMELA. I have only two sports, drinking and smoking. And if I could do them without lifting my arm, I would.

BINGHAM. You don't play, do you Louise?

---

*Here and in the space two lines later, theaters should insert the names of local worthies who are familiar to and beloved of the theatre's particular audience – the local mayor, perhaps, or the school board chairman – someone who will be known to the local audience night after night. For example, at the world premiere of the play at the Signature Theatre in Arlington, Virginia, I used the name of the theater's Artistic Director and it was one of the biggest laughs in the play.

LOUISE. No. I mean I did for a while but I gave it up. The day I started beating Justin I thought well this is no good for the relationship. I'm no dummy.

(BINGHAM *and* PAMELA *look at each other. It sinks in.*)

PAMELA. You beat Justin?

LOUISE. Yeah.

BINGHAM. At golf?

LOUISE. Yeah. He says I have a natural swing.

PAMELA. And what did you shoot? Normally. On a good round.

LOUISE. 68, 69.

BINGHAM. *(springing into action) Well why didn't you tell us?!!*

LOUISE. Me? What for?

BINGHAM. To replace Justin! What's the matter with you?! You couldn't say anything?!

LOUISE. Mr. Bingham, I hate to contradict you and all, but I'm a girl.

BINGHAM. So what?

LOUISE. It's a man's tournament.

PAMELA. It is not a man's tournament, it's a tournament!

LOUISE. But women don't play in it.

BINGHAM. Because usually they can't score as well as men, so they don't try out!

LOUISE. Are you sure?

BINGHAM. Of course I'm sure!

PAMELA. A few years ago a woman player competed on the men's tour. She lost, but she had a right to play.

LOUISE. So you're saying I could replace Justin?

PAMELA. Exactly.

LOUISE. Well what are we waiting for?! Let's go!

BINGHAM. No wait, wait, wait! Here, take this!

(*He hands her a putter and a ball.*)

PAMELA. Henry, there isn't time!

BINGHAM. Louise, take this ball and hit the leg of that blue chair.

LOUISE. The one way over there through the door?

BINGHAM. Yes!

> (**LOUISE** *throws the golf ball into the other room and we hear a loud crash of glass, as though she's thrown it into a huge mirror.*)

That's good enough, you're on. Now *move, move!* Go to the pro shop and pick an outfit and clubs and be back here in 6 minutes!

LOUISE. Yes sir!

PAMELA. Come on!

LOUISE. *Wait!* Don't I have to be a member of the club or somethin'?!

BINGHAM. She's right.

PAMELA. She's right.

> *(The next section goes very fast:)*

BINGHAM. I hereby nominate Louise Heindbedder

PAMELA. to membership in Quail Valley

BINGHAM. Golf and Country Club

PAMELA. to hold sacred

BINGHAM. its rules

PAMELA. and forever

BINGHAM. its spirit

PAMELA. and honor

BINGHAM. its code

PAMELA. amen.

BINGHAM. I second.

PAMELA. Vote?

BINGHAM. Aye.

PAMELA. Aye.

BINGHAM. You're elected.

BINGHAM & PAMELA. Chucka, chucka, chucka, *go, go, go!!*

(As LOUISE *and* PAMELA *exit,* DICKIE *reenters.)*

DICKIE. Well? Do you have a name of the replacement yet or should I take out my sundial.

BINGHAM. I do have a name, and you can put your sundial back where the sunlight can't find it.

DICKIE. Oh I don't know why you bother, Bingham. That's what I should start calling you, Mr. "Why-Bother-Bingham." You're just prolonging the agony, Henry.

BINGHAM. We are playing a replacement, Dickie, now go tell the Starter.

DICKIE. All right, I'll tell him. And what's the name of this magnificent golfer you have signed up out of thin air. Wait, don't tell me, it's Ben Hogan, you've brought him back from the dead. Or Byron Nelson. Or Sam Sneed?

BINGHAM. Her name is Louise Heindbedder.

DICKIE. It's a woman?

BINGHAM. That's right.

DICKIE. Well I know it's not against the rules, but is this really necessary? You think a woman is going to beat Tramplemain?

BINGHAM. Why don't you just leave that to me.

DICKIE. Fine, fine. Do as you please.

(He heads for the door and pauses.)

She is a member, I take it.

BINGHAM. Yes.

DICKIE. *(suspicious)* Nominated? Voted on?

*(*LOUISE *enters, followed by* PAMELA. LOUISE *is wearing a nifty golf outfit and carrying her clubs.)*

LOUISE. "And when the rival gods
Took up their Nike drivers with the
High-density forged-alloy heads
The Earth did tremble at the
Thought of such a battle!"

DICKIE. This is the young lady?

BINGHAM. That's right.

DICKIE. And she's a member here?

BINGHAM. Yes I told you that.

DICKIE. Excuse me, Miss, but when were you elected to this club?

LOUISE. *(proudly)* Today.

DICKIE. And you applied for membership when, exactly?!

LOUISE. *(glances at* **BINGHAM** *and* **PAMELA** *for help)* ...Today?

DICKIE. So you did not have to wait twelve months for membership, so therefore you must be related to someone else at this club, *and who pray tell is that, if you don't mind?!!*

PAMELA. ...She's my daughter.

DICKIE. Oh, I see. Your daughter. The one I've never heard of before.

PAMELA. That's right.

DICKIE. Oh, please, must you insult my intelligence this way?

PAMELA. Aside from the obvious reply about your intelligence, you simply can't prove otherwise.

DICKIE. Of course I can. Miss Heindbedder, is this your mother? Look me in the eye. Tell me the truth! *Look me in the eye!*

*(***LOUISE***'s lip starts to quiver.)*

BINGHAM. Oh stop it, Dickie. Leave her alone! She's just a kid.

DICKIE. Oh dear, oh dear, is this compassion I hear from Henry Bingham? What have we here? Is it a whole new man? What has changed you, Henry? The love of a good woman, like in the movies? Oh, I can hear the violins now! "You have changed me, Pamela-la-la-la,-la, and my heart-heart-heart-heart is brimming over with love-love-love-love and caring-ing-ing-ing-ing!"

LOUISE. You're such a terrible man. You're really terrible. I wasn't going to lie. The truth is I was adopted and I don't know who my birth-mother was so maybe it *is* Mrs. Peabody. And do you know what? You really can't prove she isn't!

DICKIE. Oh, please, don't be ridiculous! I will *find* your "birth parents" if necessary! There are two hundred thousand dollars at stake!

LOUISE. *Well go ahead and try, but you'll never find 'em! Because the only hint I have about my birth-parents is this birthmark on my shoulder shaped like a small purple flower.*

(PAMELA *staggers backward.*)

And I have a bigger one on my backside, too.

PAMELA. Oh my God. Let me see it.

(LOUISE *starts pulling her shorts down.*)

No, the one on your shoulder!

LOUISE. *(pulling her sleeve over her shoulder)* I've had it since I was a baby.

(PAMELA *gasps.*)

PAMELA. Look at this.

(PAMELA *pulls down her own sleeve and shows* LOUISE *the identical birthmark.* LOUISE *is speechless.*)

When were you adopted?

LOUISE. March 8th, 1985. I was eight days old.

PAMELA. I gave birth to a daughter on March 1st, 1985. I was an unwed mother.

LOUISE. My birth-mother was unwed.

PAMELA. I have hazel eyes.

LOUISE. And so do I.

PAMELA. I'm nearsighted.

LOUISE. And so am I!

PAMELA. I'm allergic to makeup except Donna Karan's Spring Dazzler Collection and my favorite color is

PAMELA & LOUISE. *Sandstorm Blue!!*

LOUISE. *Mommy!*

PAMELA. *Lou-Lou!*

(*They embrace.*)

LOUISE. This is just like a Greek play or somethin'! And what about my birth-father? Do you stay in touch with him?!

PAMELA. You're not going to believe this.

(*She looks at* BINGHAM.)

BINGHAM. ...Jesus Christ.

PAMELA. Don't you remember? Graduation night?

BINGHAM. I thought I was shooting blanks!

LOUISE. Daddy!!

BINGHAM. Girl-child!

(*They embrace.* DICKIE *exits in disgust.*)

LOUISE. (*wiping her eyes*) Oh I can't wait till you meet my real mom and dad, the ones who raised me, they're the best people in the whole world and you're going to love them *so much!*

PAMELA. I'm sure we will.

BINGHAM. It will be a very important moment in our lives, and I'll congratulate them on raising such a wonderful daughter, and we'll all be very moved and touched *but will you please get the hell outside before we lose the WHOLE GOD DAMN MATCH!!*

LOUISE. *Let's go!!!*

(*As the three of them run out of the room,* JUSTIN *runs in through another entrance. His arm is in a sling, his hair is askew and he's taken so many pain-killers that he's totally loopy. He's carrying a large wrench and a plumber's tool box.*)

JUSTIN. Louise! Louise, I have the best idea in the entire world! I can find the ring! It's not a problem! You flushed it down the toilet! I'm good with toilets!

(*The phone rings.*)

JUSTIN. *(cont.)* Hello?…The hospital?!…*Who* escaped?!…
Well of course he shouldn't be loose with all that med-
ication in him. He could be dangerous!

*(He hangs up and plops down on the sofa where – some-
where in his addled mind full of pain-killer fantasy – he's
being interviewed by Oprah Winfrey.)*

JUSTIN. Well, Oprah, I'm from a family of plumbers. My dad
was a plumber. My grandfather. And my guess is that the
engagement ring that my fiancée lost is still down there
in the toilet where she flushed it! So, in the immortal
words of my grandfather as he lowered himself into his
first septic tank: I SHALL RETURN! Hahahahahaha!

*(***JUSTIN*** runs out the door – and smacks straight into the
wall with a loud crack. He screams with pain, then he
runs out the door, this time successfully.)*

*(Inspiring golf music starts to play, the kind they play on
The Golf Channel when a new day of golf is being broad-
cast.)*

*(Simultaneously, THE FRONT OF THE STAGE IS
MAGICALLY TRANSFORMED INTO THE 18TH
GREEN UNDER A BRIGHT BLUE SKY.)**

(As the change occurs, we hear the **STARTER** *through the
outdoor PA System.)*

STARTER. *(offstage)* Welcome back ladies and gentlemen to
the 43rd Annual Tournament between Quail Valley
Golf and Country Club and Crouching Squirrel Golf
and Racquet Club. The score is now tied between the
two clubs, and play has resumed on the final hole of the
tournament, the par 3 Eighteenth…

---

* Note: This change can be as large or small as the theater desires. It can
be done as simply as turning over the downstage rug in the tap room
(so that the rug is now green) and changing the lighting to a nice sunny
dappled effect (which is how I originally imagined the change). Or a
curtain could be dropped behind the actors showing the expanse of the
golf course. Or, as in the premiere production, the set could slide apart
to reveal the 18th green with the clubhouse on either side. Any of these
approaches will work equally well as long as the transition feels seamless
and doesn't hold up the action.

(The voice of the STARTER *begins fading along with the lights.)*

...where a new player for Quail Valley, Miss Louise Heindbedder, is stepping up to the tee where she will play in competition with Mr. Steve Tramplemain, making this one of the most unusual sporting events in the history of Quail Valley Golf and Country Club...*

(We hear the sound of applause and the lights come up on the 18th green fifteen minutes later.)

STARTER. ...and good luck to Miss Heindbedder as she approaches the green with one, final chance to win this tournament.

*(*LOUISE *now strides onto the green as* PAMELA, BINGHAM, DICKIE, *and* MURIEL *hurry to the side of the green to join the gallery.)*

BINGHAM. Did you see Tramplemain? He was terrific. He holed out with a 74!

PAMELA. Yes, I know, but if she makes this putt she wins the whole thing!

BINGHAM. Yes, but it's 90 feet.

PAMELA. Well, it's only one putt.

BINGHAM. Only one...are you insane? That's a quarter of a football field!

MURIEL. Shhh!

DICKIE. There's a lot of break in that putt.

MURIEL. Oh, be quiet!

PAMELA. Did we ask for your opinion?!

*(*LOUISE *sizes up the putt by crouching and letting her putter dangle from her fingertips, then lying out spread eagle, etc.)*

DICKIE. It has three breaks, actually, one for each level of the –

---

*Note: If the golf green is in place before this speech is over, please shorten it so that the action stays as tight and continuous as possible.

BINGHAM. Would you shut up!

> (*LOUISE is ready.*)
>
> (*She does her pre-shot routine...stands behind the putt... she's ready to make the swing...*)
>
> (*When* **JUSTIN** *rushes onto the green.*)

JUSTIN. *(waving the ring)* Louise, guess what?!

LOUISE. *Justin!*

BINGHAM. Oh my God –

PAMELA. Oh, no –

LOUISE. Justin, sweetheart, this is the tournament.

JUSTIN. Of course it is, but I've got to show you something. As it says in the Bible, *"Weeping may tarry for a night, BUT JOY COMETH IN THE MORNING!"*

> (*singing*)

"Let me sing a happy song, With crazy words that roll along – "

LOUISE. Justin, please –

DICKIE. I love that boy.

MURIEL. Be quiet!

JUSTIN. You're gonna go nuts, I promise, just look!

BINGHAM. Justin, get out of there!

PAMELA. No, let the officials deal with it.

BINGHAM. But they're not here!

MURIEL. *Officials! Come! Officials!*

JUSTIN. *(trying to take* **LOUISE***'s putter)* Louise, just put down the putter!

LOUISE. No!

> (*They struggle over the putter.*)

JUSTIN. It'll make you happy!

LOUISE. Justin, stop it!

JUSTIN. You don't need the putter!

LOUISE. *It's my putter, now cut it out!*

(They end up with JUSTIN *behind* LOUISE, *with his arms wrapped around her body – and as the putter flails wildly in front of them, it accidentally strikes the ball and sends it zooming across the green.)*

(Whack!)

(Gasp!)

LOUISE. *(cont.)* Oh, Justin!!

PAMELA. Oh my God!

BINGHAM. They hit it!

MURIEL. There it goes!

(They all stare intently off stage, following the path of the ball.)

DICKIE. There's the first break…

(Gasp.)

PAMELA. That wasn't too bad, was it?

BINGHAM. It's hard to tell.

MURIEL. It's gaining speed –

DICKIE. There's the second break!

(Gasp.)

MURIEL. It's slowing down…

BINGHAM. Come on, come on…

PAMELA. Keep rolling, you sucker…

MURIEL. Keep rolling…

(Ah!)

BINGHAM. *(grabbing* PAMELA *happily)* It made the hill!

PAMELA. It's heading for the cup!

MURIEL. *(grabbing* DICKIE*)* Another ten feet ..!

DICKIE. No, no –

BINGHAM. Come on –

PAMELA. *Come on…*

MURIEL. *Get in the cup, GET IN THE CUP!!…*

(*A moment of silence as everyone stares and agonizes... Then we hear the sound of a ball rolling around and around...and into the cup.*)

BINGHAM, PAMELA, LOUISE, JUSTIN & MURIEL. *YES! YES! YES! YES! HA HAAAAAAAA! YES! YES!*

(**LOUISE** *is hugging* **JUSTIN** *and dancing around the green happily.* **BINGHAM** *hugs* **PAMELA** *and twirls her around.* **DICKIE** *sits gloomily at the side of the green.*)

JUSTIN. Louise, Louise listen to me! I have a surprise for you! Ta da!

(*He holds up the ring.* **LOUISE** *gasps and her heart skips a beat.*)

LOUISE. Is it really Granny's?

JUSTIN. I come from a long line of plumbers. It was still in the U-bend.

LOUISE. Oh, Justin, I...

(*She's about to take it from him...then:*)

Did you rinse it off?

(*He nods.*)

Oh, Justin!

(*She puts it on and they embrace.*)

MURIEL. Well at least I have my shop back.

DICKIE. Poor Muriel, she's been through a lot today.

MURIEL. As if you care.

DICKIE. I do. I feel some strange connection to you. I have for years.

MURIEL. I think it's your sweaters.

DICKIE. You mean you *like* them?

MURIEL. Of course I like them. I knitted them for you.

DICKIE. ...Scaramouche?

MURIEL. Boom. Right down the middle.

DICKIE. Oh my God, I think I'm in love with you!

MURIEL. You will be when I get through with you. Henry, I want a divorce.

BINGHAM. Yes! Ha-haaa!…Oh, Muriel, I'm so sorry…

MURIEL. Oh Henry, stop your nonsense. Will you be all right?

BINGHAM. Well, let's see now. We've won the tournament, so I get to keep my job. I have discovered that I have the daughter whom I've longed for all my life. And I have declared my love for the woman I adore, not only to her but in front of the entire membership of Quail Valley Golf and Country Club. The only question now is whether she'll marry me.

(He kneels.)

PAMELA. …Let me think. I've been married three times, and every time to the wrong man. I actually found the right man first crack out of the box, but I didn't realize it until it was too late. You've been the man of my dreams for as long as I can remember, and you just won two hundred thousand dollars in cash. Of course I'll marry you, darling, we're in love!

*(They laugh and embrace as **LOUISE** steps forward.)*

*(Stirring Scottish music begins to play. The lights change slowly during the following speech, picking out each of our heroes, then **LOUISE** especially. By the final stanza, **LOUISE** is illuminated in the bright, warm glow of hope for the future.)*

LOUISE. And now, at close of play,
We see how the gods themselves,
Both clear-eyed Venus and the warrior Mars,
Did assist Quail Valley in its quest for victory,
A victory that shall live in song and story
As long as duffers shank their shots and
Champions stride the fairways of their Mother Earth.
And now we ask, like Homer,
Who was old and wise and blind,
If there is Moral to be taken from this test of courage;
And behold there is, and it is this:

LOUISE. *(cont.)* Stay the course,
    O stay the course,
    Do not give up in fear,
    And never want for fellowship
    And never want for cheer.
    With every game in life you play
    Go forward to the light,
    And play with joy and honor,
    And we wish you all good night.

Curtain

CURTAIN CALL

Before the traditional final bows, the cast now pantomimes their way through the entire play at top speed to the great finale of the *William Tell Overture* by Rossini. The music should begin with the famous "Lone Ranger" trumpet fanfare; it should then be shortened from its original three minutes to about 90-100 seconds in order to make the pantomime feel as compact and frantic as possible.

I came up with this idea in connection with another one of my plays, *Lend Me A Tenor*, when it was first produced in London. I then imported the curtain call into the Broadway production, and it has become a sort of hallmark of that play ever since. I have always wanted to repeat the device as part of one of my other comedies, and this seemed like the right one.

A scenario describing the action of the curtain call is set forth below. The action is divided into numbered paragraphs for the sake of convenience in rehearsal; however, the action is intended to flow continuously from beginning to end without a pause, with the actors literally running from one place to the next. Also, the actors should feel free to play their "moments" in the curtain call more broadly than in the play proper so that the story of the play emerges as clearly as possible.

To avoid confusion, it should be noted that in some instances, entrances and exits occur through different doors than they do in the play proper and that, in condensing the story to 90 seconds, some portions of the action have been consciously omitted. A few props will have to be pre-set before the curtain call can begin. However, the curtain call should explode into action as soon as possible after the play is ended.

One important note for the cast: in order to make this curtain call work to maximum effect, you should never make it look easy, no matter how many times you've done it. Always run from one set piece to the next and make the audience feel that you are making it there just barely in time. Especially at the end, make it feel like you're reaching that final moment without a second to spare. This makes the spectators feel like the one and only audience who have seen the impossible take place before their eyes. Indeed, some member or two of the cast should give a shout of relief at the final moment just before the blackout.

Finally, the director should feel free to change the action of the curtain call, where necessary, to reflect any specific business that may be added to the particular production. The idea is to present the visual high points of the production just seen. Thus, every curtain call for *Lend Me A Tenor* has differed slightly from every other one over the years, and I'm hoping for the same lovely fate for *The Fox on the Fairway*.

SCENARIO

Notes to the Scenario

(1) Dickie's series of sweaters for the curtain call should include as many new ones as the theater can manage. The next-to-last one might be just a front with Velcro, so he can pull it off in full view and reveal the final awful sweater. (2) Other than Dickie's sweaters, there are no costume changes during the curtain call because there is no time for them. (3) The curtain call is entirely pantomimed. No one speaks or even shouts except in mime – except at the very end, when one or more cast members can hoot with the joy because they've just made it into the last pose to coincide with the last bar of music (see advice above). (4) You may find that you can only get a portion of these "moments" below into the curtain call in the 90 seconds of the music that have been allotted. That's fine. Just pick the ones that tell the story from beginning to end and finish up with the final putt and the jump into each others' arms. However it's done, it will be exhilarating.

Scenario

1. Justin and Louise chase each other around the set. Justin proposes and they make out. Bingham enters, Louise and Justin react, and Louise runs off.

2. Bingham kisses Trampelmain's picture as Dickie enters in his first awful sweater. As Justin exits, Bingham and Dickie shake hands on the bet. As Dickie exits, Bingham sinks down in the chair with the letter, reacting as he does in the play.

3. Pamela enters and joins Bingham to watch Justin through the window as he hits his drives. Justin enters apologetically.

4. Bingham sets a ball on the rug and Justin putts at the chair through the hall. Bingham gives Justin his pep talk and they run out in opposite directions.

5. Dickie runs on in his second awful sweater. Pamela reacts to the sweater, then Bingham enters and reacts to the sweater, and Dickie exits.

6. Justin and Louise rushes on. Justin is in a golf cap to represent the new golf outfit. Louise delivers her Homeric ode. Justin does a push-up and Louise and Justin rush off.

7. Pamela and Bingham rush to the window, watch Justin's shot and hug each other.

8. Bingham exits as Louise enters. She mimes "I lost ring my engagement ring!" Louise runs off and Pamela runs after her.

9. Bingham and Justin run in. They pantomime the "Ommmm" and "Chucka" moments, then Bingham exits as Louise runs on and mimes to Justin "I lost the ring." Justin reacts.

10. Pamela runs in, they all weep together. Bingham runs in, sees them and reacts.

11. Louis gets mad at Justin and rushes out. Pamela follows her as Bingham gets out the vase and gives it to Justin. Louise runs in followed by Pamela. Louise grabs the vase and makes a run for it. The vase gets tossed around. [This could be shortened to just throwing the vase around.]

12. Pamela kisses Justin. Louise sees it and reacts, at which point Pamela is hit with hysterical blindness and winds up in Bingham's arms.

13. Muriel enters and hits Bingham with newspaper. Dickie enters and Pamela punches Dickie.

14. Pamela and Muriel push each other, then Muriel marches Justin out the door.

15. Pamela, Bingham and Dickie watch Justin drive ball into the water. "AAHH!!!" Pamela and Dickie run off while Bingham holds up a sign that says "Intermission."

16. Pamela and Bingham enter and clink champagne glasses, then Bingham grabs the bullhorn and makes the announcement to the party.

17. Bingham and Pamela exit as Louise enters carrying large sign that says "sexy red dress" and shimmies behind it.

18. Dickie and Muriel enter, Dickie in his 3rd awful sweater. They kiss and run off.

19. Pamela and Bingham enter drunk. Pamela lays on the floor and puckers. Bingham takes a swing; then Pamela jumps up and does her oyster dance.

20. Bingham woos Pamela; "The PA's still on!" Muriel enters with golf club and hits the amplifier. Dickie enters in 4th awful sweater, then Justin and Louise enter from the kitchen with their shirts pulled up to their chins. Dickie pulls off front of sweater to reveal another awful sweater underneath.

21. Justin grabs golf club, hits the box with the vase, breaks his arm and they all react.

22. Justin, Louise and Dickie exit as Bingham, Muriel and Pamela pose in their thinking position. Muriel exits as Louise enters and poses in the "I'm no dummy" moment and Pamela and Bingham react. She throws the ball through the door.

23. Dickie enters as Louise pulls on golf cap and poses, reciting the Homeric ode.

24. Louise and Pamela compare birth marks and embrace. Then Louise and Bingham embrace.

25. They all exit as Justin enters with tool box, "I found the ring!"

26. Everyone rushes on and poses for the final putt. Justin and Louise hit the ball. Everyone looks out, reacting to the putt, the ball drops in the hole, and Pamela, Muriel and Louise jump into the arms of Bingham, Dickie and Justin.

"Yes!"

Blackout

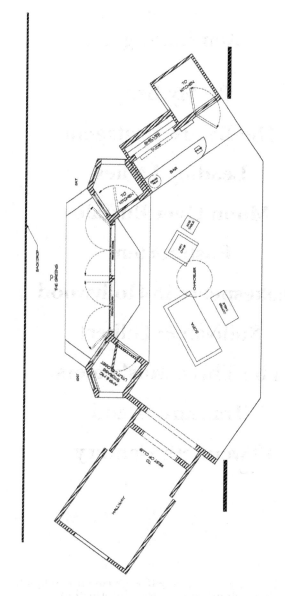

FOX ON THE FAIRWAY

BY KEN LUDWIG
SET DESIGN BY JAMES KRONZER
SIGNATURE THEATER

ACT 1, SCENE 1: TAP ROOM OF THE QUAIL VALLEY COUNTRY CLUB

KEN LUDWIG has had six shows on Broadway and seven in London's West End, and his plays and musicals have been performed in more than 30 countries in over twenty languages. His first play on Broadway, *Lend Me A Tenor*, which the *Washington Post* called "one of the classic comedies of the 20th century," won two Tony Awards and was nominated for seven. He has also won two Laurence Olivier Awards (England's highest theater honor), the Charles MacArthur Award, two Helen Hayes Awards, the Edgar Award for Best Mystery from The Mystery Writers of America, the SETC Distinguished Career Award, and the Edwin Forrest Award for Services to the American Theatre. His plays have been commissioned by the Royal Shakespeare Company and the Bristol Old Vic. He has written 23 plays and musicals, including *Crazy For You* (five years on Broadway and the West End, Tony and Olivier Award Winner for Best Musical), *Moon Over Buffalo* (Broadway and West End), *The Adventures of Tom Sawyer* (Broadway), *Treasure Island* (West End), *Twentieth Century* (Broadway), *Baskerville, Leading Ladies, Shakespeare in Hollywood, The Game's Afoot, The Fox on the Fairway, The Three Musketeers* and *The Beaux' Stratagem*. His play *A Comedy of Tenors* was chosen to mark the 100th Anniversary of the Cleveland Playhouse and was co-produced by the McCarter Theatre. His newest book, *How To Teach Your Children Shakespeare*, won The Falstaff Award for Best Shakespeare Book of 2014 and is published by Random House. His plays have starred Alec Baldwin, Carol Burnett, Lynn Redgrave, Mickey Rooney, Hal Holbrook, Dixie Carter, Tony Shalhoub, Anne Heche, Joan Collins, and Kristin Bell. His work is published by the Yale Review, and he is a Sallie B. Goodman Fellow of the McCarter Theatre. He holds degrees from Harvard, where he studied music with Leonard Bernstein, Haverford College and Cambridge University. For more information, please visit www.kenludwig.com.